A GOOD BAD IDEA NOVEL

ARIELLA ZOELLE

Copyright © 2020 A.F. Zoelle/Ariella Zoelle

Published by Sarayashi Publishing

www.ariellazoelle.com

All rights reserved.

This is a work of fiction. Names, characters, places, and incidents are products of the author's imagination or used fictitiously. Any resemblance to actual persons, living or dead, is purely coincidental. All products and brand names are registered trademarks of their respective holders/companies.

This book or any portion thereof may not be reproduced or used in any manner whatsoever without the express written permission of the publisher except for the use of brief quotations in a book review.

Cover Design by Cate of Cate Ashwood Designs

Editing by Pam of Undivided Editing

Proofreading by Sandra of One Love Editing

Layout by Ariella of Sarayashi Publishing

ISBN: 978-1-7324473-6-3

Dedication

For everyone who loves a smart-ass (and thinks the dictionary needs to change the spelling to smartass), this one is for you.

Author's Note

The **Good Bad Idea** series can be read in any order. However, if you would like to see where Xander's story began, please refer to Chapter 8 of **Bet on Love**. Jules first appears in Chapters 1, 2, 4, 5, and 10 of **Fancy Love**. This book starts one week before the epilogue of Bet on Love.

Welcome to Sunnyside!

Immerse yourself in the world of interconnected series set in the fictional town of Sunnyside

Full of cute sweetness and sexy fun, every story ends with a satisfying HEA and no cliffhangers. Since all of the following series are set in the same town, you can expect to see cameos of your favorite characters! The books are funny, steamy, and can be read in any order.

To access the Sunnyside universe reading order guide, please visit www.ariellazoelle.com/sunnyside

Chapter One

XANDER

AFTER DEALING with my umpteenth disaster for the day, I had officially had it. Today could go fuck itself. So could tomorrow. I was done with everything.

The only thing that would make me feel better would be getting pounded into the mattress until I forgot about what was wrong. But I had broken up with my boyfriend, Josh, last week after I found out he had been cheating on me for two months, so that wasn't happening. *Asshole.*

Since I couldn't fuck away my stress, I went to my best friend's apartment instead. Jules was the only person who could make me laugh, even when I was ready to burn down the world around me. He was the one constant in my life I could count on to never let me down. I could indulge my messy emotions around him without having to maintain my flawless facade of always being cool, calm, and collected. He was the only one who knew how exhausting it was for me to be perfect and make everything look easy all the time.

Jules opened the door, grinning when he saw me. He looked better in his faded jeans and lavender shirt than anyone had the right to. His mussed blond hair, bright blue eyes, and laid-back attitude about all things made him quite charming. Without that, he'd never be able to put up with me being so uptight. Being inseparable best friends since we were eight also helped. "Is there some reason you look like you want to murder me?"

"Just shut up and hug me."

My best friend enjoyed hugging as much as most people liked sex. He didn't need to be told twice. After he kicked the door closed, he pulled me into a tight embrace without questioning my need for it or getting mad at me for being bossy. For some reason, that never seemed to bother him.

I wrapped my arms around him, resting my head on his shoulder with a heavy sigh. For the first time since I woke up, the tightness in my chest loosened, and I could breathe again. It meant I could smell his perfume, which he always wore instead of cologne. His logic was they designed it to attract men to women, so it should bring them to him. I used to tease him for it, but I stopped after witnessing it succeed with countless guys over the years. Rather than arouse me, the unique blend of berries, patchouli, and cedar comforted me with its familiarity.

Jules rubbed my back without saying a word. For someone who could talk your ear off, he was surprisingly intuitive about when to be quiet. His calmness helped center me from the chaos that controlled my mind. He really gave the best hugs in the world.

My jaw unclenched as I relaxed into his hold. However, weariness set in as my anger subsided. It made me wish we could curl up together to get some proper sleep. I had slept like shit every night since I had kicked Josh out of our apartment. The idea tempted me, especially because Jules would do anything for me. It was probably weird that I was comfortable enough with my best friend to be fine with a platonic cuddle session, but I was too exhausted to care. I needed sleep more than I needed to respect the social boundaries of acceptable behavior amongst male friends. "Can we do this in bed?"

"Are you seriously asking to snuggle with me?" he asked in an amused tone.

I stepped out of his hold with an annoyed huff. "Listen. I've had a shitty day, I'm dead-ass tired, and I know it's weird, but it would help me feel better. Please?"

"Wow, I never thought you'd beg me to sleep with you," he teased. I gave him a pained look, which made him turn serious. "I'll agree on one condition."

"Which is?"

"You have to tell me what's bothering you."

It was a small price to pay for comfort. "Deal."

His eyebrows arched in surprise. "No argument or bartering? Really?" I crossed my arms over my chest with an unamused frown. "Fine, I'll quit torturing you. Come on."

I admired that nothing ever seemed to faze Jules. He was the only person I knew who wouldn't bat an eyelash at my strange request. Without a word, I followed him into his bedroom.

It looked like a fight had broken out at a yard sale, with clothes strewn all over the floor at the foot of his bed. His room was as messy now at thirty-three years old as it was when we were teenagers. Some things never changed.

"I can feel you judging me," he said with a grin. "It's not *that* bad."

The state of his laundry was beyond my concern. I stripped down to my pants and undershirt, then crawled under his maroon comforter. Once he got in bed, I curled up next to him and used his shoulder for a pillow. I sprawled over him with natural ease, hooking my leg over his and draping my arm across his chest, as if this was something we did all the time. It got even better when he wrapped his arms around me to hold me close. Surrounded by his reassuring scent, I melted against him as all my stress finally left me. For the first time since my breakup, I finally felt at peace. It was magical.

He had the decency to give me a few moments of

silence before asking, "What happened?"

"I'm never getting married."

"It's only been a week since your breakup with Josh, so don't say—"

I cut him off before he could finish. "No, this is about Rhys." A year ago, my boss went to Las Vegas to marry his heinous fiancée, Olivia. Instead, he eloped with his best friend, Lucien St. Amour. To celebrate their first anniversary, they were having a second wedding for their friends and family to share in their joy. "His wedding planner had some kind of family crisis this week, which means I have to keep dealing with shit."

"Does Rhys know?"

"No, I can't stress him out with this nonsense." The extra work was annoying, but I still cared about my boss. He was one of the most generous and giving people I had ever met. I wanted everything to be perfect for him. "The wedding planner thinks he'll be back next week, but a lot of shit needs done between now and then. If I don't take care of it, it won't be right."

"What about Callum?"

He was referring to my assistant, who also was Jules's younger brother's boyfriend. I hadn't been sure at first about working with someone so young, but Callum was meticulous with details and eager to help with any project I gave him. The word "no" wasn't in his vocabulary with work. He was a lifesaver, and I was grateful that Rhys had found somebody so well suited for me. "I feel bad he keeps putting in so much overtime with wedding stuff. Rune must hate me for monopolizing Callum's time this week."

"He's in Italy for a photo shoot, which is probably why Callum volunteered to put in extra hours. Rune comes home tomorrow, though. I'm having dinner at his place on Sunday."

Once he said that, it jogged my memory. It wasn't like me to forget details. Damn, I was struggling more than I realized. "That's right, he mentioned that."

As always, Jules highlighted the bright side of the situation. "Look at it this way. It'll be good practice for him when he marries my brother someday."

Rune had spent most of his life being a loner, so I was happy he had found love with Callum. I tried not to be envious after yet another failed romance. There went six years of my life down the drain for nothing. "Mm-hmm."

"What's actually bothering you? An incompetent wedding planner wouldn't get you this worked up normally."

Damn him for knowing me so well. Some of my earlier irritation encroached on my solace I found being next to my best friend. "Josh is still coming to Rhys's wedding."

"Why does that asshole think he gets to be your plus-one after you broke up?" Jules demanded, his tone becoming defensive. He had never hidden his distaste for my ex-boyfriend. The reason for our split had only made it more vitriolic.

"Because he's going as the date of one of Rhys's attorneys." Bile rose in my throat at the thought of having to see the two men together. The whole situation was strange, because I genuinely liked Elias enough to feel bad for him. It was obvious Josh was using him as a stepping-stone to further his career.

They were both lawyers on our in-house legal team. While Elias's father was the lead counsel, he had worked hard to earn his place. Rhys had hand-picked Elias to work on his projects as general counsel, while Josh was on a different team as assistant general counsel. One of the managing counsel attorneys had announced her plans to retire in a few months, and my ex was obsessed with getting that promotion. It was a pipe dream given the number of more qualified candidates available, but that never stopped his ambition.

Josh would do anything to get ahead, which apparently included fucking Elias. His logic was so simplistic. In his mind, dating the son of the person in charge of hiring the new managing counsel would give him the leg up he needed to secure the promotion. Not that it was some great hardship. Elias was cute as hell and was so kind that I couldn't understand how he ended up a corporate lawyer. He deserved better than being manipulated by my ex-boyfriend.

I didn't want to be sympathetic toward the person

Josh cheated on me with, but Elias had no way of knowing about our history. Because I preferred to be discreet, we had kept our relationship a secret at work. Besides, everyone at my office assumed I was dating Jules, so it would reflect poorly on me that people thought I was cheating on him with Josh. That was the other reason Elias wouldn't have known I was Josh's boyfriend. I hated that I couldn't be mad at him. No matter how much I wanted to blame him, it wasn't his fault that my ex stepped out on me. He would find out soon enough that he was being used. Karma was a bitch like that.

The only person who deserved my wrath was Josh. I should have been angrier about him cheating on me for the last two months, but our relationship had broken down so much by that point that I didn't even have the energy to give a shit. Besides, he hadn't put me at risk since the last time we had fucked was in December. He kept claiming he was too tired for it. I guess now I knew the reason why; he was too busy hooking up with Elias. If I was being honest with myself, it was a relief to finally have a reason to leave him. Why had I stayed so long in such a shitty relationship?

Jules pulled me back to the present when he growled, "Oh, that is bullshit!"

His outrage on my behalf comforted me. "There's nothing I can do about it. If I fight Josh about it, he wins. My only choice is to grin and bear it."

"No, fuck that. This requires revenge."

The vindictive part of me was all for that plan, but I had to be realistic. "And how would you propose I do that without ruining Rhys's special day?"

"Since you're the de facto wedding planner, you're in charge of the guest list, right? You have the power to ban that asshole from coming, so use it."

It was a nice thought but impractical. "I refuse to give him the satisfaction of knowing his presence bothers me that much." That's when something occurred to me. "Wait, you know what bothered him the most?"

"That you were too good for him?"

"No, he's convinced I'm in love with you. It drove him crazy with jealousy for years."

Jules scoffed. "He always was more pretty than smart."

I chuckled as an idea formed in my mind. "What would really get under his skin is seeing me happy with you. If you attend the wedding as my date, it'll be a fair fight."

To my surprise, he didn't immediately agree. "Do you want the other people you work with to think I'm your boyfriend?"

"Everyone already assumes we're dating, so what's the harm? Rhys likes you, plus Callum and Rune will be there. If you come, we can have fun, especially if we get a little payback in the process."

"Are you sure this is a good idea?"

"It's a *fantastic* idea," I insisted. "You don't want to help me exact some vengeance against Josh for cheating on me after six years? Getting revenge was your suggestion in the first place."

"If you want him to buy it, you need to sell it. Are you prepared to do that?"

It was too easy to tease him back. "I'm already in bed with you. I can survive holding your hand in public if it means pissing off my ex. It's not like we have to make out in front of him to get the point across."

Jules was silent for a long moment before saying, "I'm game, if that's what you want."

Satisfied I had gotten my way, I nuzzled against him with a contented noise. "Thank you, Julie." I only called him that when I felt extra affectionate. Whereas if he was in trouble, I used his full name, Julian. "I appreciate you indulging me being unreasonable."

He hugged me closer, brushing my upper arm with his thumb. The intimate gesture sent a shiver of pleasure through me. I had to remind my body that wasn't what I was after. "You know I would do anything for you, Xan."

There was no question about that. It should have set off warning alarms that being held by him made me feel more loved than I ever had been by Josh. But I was too tired and happy to hear them as I drifted to sleep.

Chapter Two

JULES

AS XANDER STOOD *in my bedroom, he held my gaze while undoing the knot of his pink tie. There was something sensual about the way he slid the fabric free to drop on the floor. It made me swallow hard as he shrugged out of his suit jacket and teal button-down shirt.*

"You know, there's one thing I miss more than cuddling."

I remained silent as he pulled off his undershirt and threw it aside. My fingers twitched with an unforgivable need to touch him, to trace the outlines of his lithe frame and make him tremble with desire. They were urges I shouldn't have about my best friend, but that didn't stop them from torturing me.

"Do you want to guess what that is?" He slid off his black slacks and stepped out of them. It left him in a bright purple jockstrap that made me hard in an instant. He turned to show off his pert ass in all of its bare glory, hugged by neon pink straps. "I bet you only need one try."

When he ran his hands over his exposed cheeks and

squeezed, I lost my tenuous grip on my self-control. I pinned him face-first against the wall, my erection pressed against temptation. My voice came out as a dark rumble as I warned him, "Don't play games me with me you aren't willing to finish, Xander."

"I'll do whatever it takes to get you to fuck me into a better mood." He rocked against my hardness. "Interested?"

I spun him around to slam his back against the wall, pinning his wrists above his head. He took advantage of the new position by rubbing his erection against me, breaking the last of my restraint. I leaned forward and kissed him hard, devouring him with years of pent-up desires I constantly denied having. He fought me for dominance, which turned me on even more. It was a fierce battle between us that left me panting and wanting for more.

As much as I wanted to keep him in place, I had to let go to rip off my clothes as fast as I could. He used the opportunity to move to the bed, resting on all fours and wiggling his ass to tempt me further. I was powerless to resist the urge to get behind him, holding his hips as I slid my rigid length between his cheeks.

Xander pushed back against me as he groaned, "Hurry up and fuck me already!"

It would be fun to tease him, but that would mean denying myself. Instead of being gentle, I gave in to what we both wanted. I shifted the thin piece of fabric to the side and started fucking him hard. Bless him for having the foresight to prepare himself before coming over. He cried out in pleasure as he braced himself on his forearms, his body keeping pace with my aggres-

sive thrusting. Our animalistic joining pushed me to new heights as I got off on the sound of our bodies connecting.

I pounded into him, loving the way it made him cry out "Julie." He shouted when I snapped one of the elastic straps on his jock against him. When Xander touched himself for relief, I grabbed his hand and held it against the bed. It earned me an aggravated growl that almost did me in, but I refused to let him up. I continued rutting against him wildly, driven by primal instincts.

He tugged to free himself, but my grip was too tight. "Please touch me, Julie! I'm so close! I need you to—goddamn it!"

Before he could complain further, I flipped him over and yanked off his underwear. His dick stood proudly, begging for attention. My mouth watered at the thought of pleasuring him orally, but that would have to wait for another time. Instead, I pushed back into him and resumed my harsh rhythm. He responded by wrapping his legs around my waist, hooking his ankles under my ass to use the leverage to his advantage.

"Show me how you touch yourself when you think of me," I ordered.

His ornery smirk was sexy as fuck. "What makes you think you're who I fantasize about when I get myself off?"

"My arrogant ego."

He laughed before taking himself in hand and putting on one hell of a show as he stroked himself. His back arched off the bed as he moaned and whimpered my name, pleading with me to let him come.

The erotic display sent me racing toward my climax. My

thrusts became erratic as I got lost in the tingle about to overtake me. "Xan!"

It was the push he needed to take him over the edge. He came all over his fist and stomach, shouting, "Julie!"

I pushed in all the way to the hilt and—

Without warning, I jerked awake. I was right on the verge of coming from my vivid sex dream. Before I could get control of myself, Xander sleepily murmuring "Julie" as his fingers stroked my bare skin under my shirt triggered my orgasm. I shuddered as I came in my underwear, overwhelmed by the memories of our rough coupling in the dream and having him curled against me in real life.

Well, *that* was embarrassing. Relief and shame warred within me, knowing it was wrong to imagine fucking my best friend, but still euphoric from my powerful release. I didn't have the wherewithal to deal with why the situation was problematic, so I ignored the guilt and focused on the afterglow instead. There was plenty of time to feel bad about it later. I'd tell myself the same lie I always did, that getting off on thoughts of Xander meant nothing and move on with my life. Just because countless people had accused me of being in love with him over the years didn't make it true. But those kinds of dreams plagued me with insidious doubts that everyone knew something I wasn't prepared to admit about myself.

Ignoring my pressing need to change into clean underwear, I held Xander closer and lost myself in the comfort I drew from holding him. It was a far better alternative than interrogating my subconscious about things best left alone.

I WOKE UP ALONE, but the sounds in my kitchen told me I wasn't the only one in my apartment. Memories of Xander coming over to visit the previous night overlapped with my sex dream, leaving me with an uncomfortable arousal that I refused to acknowledge. It was easier to think of nothing at all as I got out of bed to use the bathroom. Afterward, I changed into clean underwear, my purple rainbow unicorn pajama pants, and an aqua T-shirt.

Still bleary-eyed, I entered my kitchen where Xander was making omelets. He wore a pair of my teal "soymates" pajama bottoms. It featured a cute print of cartoon sushi and soy sauce bottles smiling at each other with tiny hearts above them. He also had on a purple ombre hoodie of mine that dwarfed his slender frame. The sight of him in my casual clothes stopped me in my tracks. He was always gorgeous, but it had been a long time since I had seen him look so boyish. Seeing him in my clothes did funny things to my heart.

The responsible part of my brain that warned me about terrible ideas seemed to have slept in. I walked over to Xander and embraced him from behind, holding him as I buried my nose against his neck. A faint hint of my perfume clung to the hoodie. There also was a lingering scent of my body wash from the shower he had taken earlier. It made him smell like *mine*. The combined effect was arousing when I wasn't in a state of mind to fend off that reaction. How could I when I hadn't even had coffee yet?

Because of my lifelong history of being an overly affectionate hugger, Xander didn't react to my actions with anything more than a warm "Good morning, Julie."

The right thing to do would be to let go of him, but it felt too good to hold him. Hugs satisfied me on a spiritual level, and I craved the closeness they brought. Nothing was better than hugging Xander, which suffused me with a sense of wholeness that no one else ever had. I had given up trying to figure out why years ago, because I didn't like any of the answers. Instead, I basked in his calmness that helped center me after the confusing dream I had. "Mornin'."

He flipped the omelet in the pan, which was a beautiful golden color. Between Xander and my brother Rune, I was spoiled with fantastic chefs in my life. It was a good thing since I was so bad at cooking. I didn't have the attention span required to make anything worth eating that took over three minutes. The microwave I caught on fire making mac and cheese in college was a flaming testament to that fact.

"Did you sleep well?"

I wondered if having a vivid sex dream about my best friend counted as sleeping well? It didn't qualify as a nightmare, but the experience left me uneasy. I hated struggling with the unbecoming need to know if I had been right about what kind of underwear Xander had on. "Yeah. You?"

He lifted a corner of the omelet with a spatula to check it. "I don't remember the last time I slept that well. Thanks for letting me stay yesterday. I really needed that."

"Anytime—"

"I wouldn't finish that sentence if I were you unless you're prepared to have me as a roommate again." He laughed as he pulled the pan off the burner to flip the omelet onto a plate. It was magazine-spread-worthy, with red and green peppers peeking out from the fluffy yellow egg, and melted cheese making it a gooey delight. There weren't any peppers or eggs in my fridge, which meant he had gone to the store so he could make us breakfast. It never ceased to amaze me that Xander could be organized enough to cook that kind of dish so early in the morning. My brain was barely functioning yet. That was the only reason that would excuse why I was one dumbass comment away from inviting him to move in and stay in my bed every night forever. I really needed to drink some coffee and stop thinking such nonsense. "You have to let go of me to eat."

The last thing I wanted to do was release him, but he was right. With a sad sigh, I stepped back from him. The loss left me bereft, but I focused my attention on preparing us the coffee he had brewed while he whipped up another omelet for himself. By the time he was ready, I was already on my second cup of coffee when we sat at my table to eat breakfast. Hopefully, it would help stop me from being so stupid.

After the first bite, I murmured in approval. "God, I forgot how good your cooking was."

"I wish I could forget how terrible yours is." We both laughed at his joke. "You're the only person I know whose cooking requires having the fire department on speed dial."

"Hey, that was one time, and it was in the middle of finals week. I hadn't slept in like three days, so I thought I added water to my mac and cheese when I didn't. The dorm called 9-1-1, not me. It was a total overreaction to a little harmless smoke."

He arched one of his elegant eyebrows at me. "And what about the ramen?"

Damn it, I forgot about the ramen. "Fine, two times. In my defense, if it takes three minutes to make on the stove, logic says it should be microwavable. How was I supposed to know it would catch on fire?"

"You never would have survived college if we hadn't lived together," Xander said with fondness. "Spending this last week alone made me miss that."

"Your piece-of-shit ex leaves you, so you spent a

week missing me being a disaster? How does that work?"

"No, I could do without the fire brigade part. The firefighters were never as sexy as the calendars promised." He warmed his hands with his coffee mug as he chuckled. "I meant living with you. No matter how shitty of a day I had, I could come home and you'd hug me and make it better like you did yesterday. I never had that with Josh, or any of my exes, if I'm being honest."

It warmed my heart to hear that Xander drew so much comfort from the thing I loved doing the most. I ached to pull him into my arms again, but I restrained myself to finishing my delicious breakfast. "You're always welcome to come over here. I'm more than happy to hug you until you can't stand it anymore."

Xander set his coffee down and continued eating. "I realized this morning that the last time I looked forward to going home was when we lived together after college. After six years of living with Josh, I dreaded having to deal with some petty bullshit drama he made up. He thought Rhys was a cruel overlord who forced me to stay at the office all hours of the night. But the truth I wasn't willing to admit to myself was that I worked all that overtime because I hated going home to him."

The question was out of my mouth before I could stop it. "If you hated being with him that much, wouldn't it have been easier to break up with the bastard than put up with that for years?" It certainly would have made my life easier not having to watch him be so upset for so many years.

His sad smile broke my heart. "You're one hundred percent right. But I was caught up in the sunk cost fallacy of it all."

"What do you mean?"

He nudged his food with his fork. "I had invested so much time and energy into my relationship with Josh, that breaking up with him would mean admitting I wasted six years of my life. My pride wouldn't let me walk away from what I thought I was supposed to want. I tried so hard not to have another failed romance, but we ended up breaking up, anyway. It was all for nothing."

As an empathetic person, Xander's misery tore me up inside. "No, it wasn't. You learned what you won't put up with, and you'll take that lesson into your next relationship. Him being an asshole will help you learn who to avoid in the future. That's about the only thing that bastard is useful for."

"Yeah, you're right." He sighed as he ruffled his chestnut-colored hair. Some strands stuck up, which enhanced his boyish charm. "I'm an idiot for ignoring all the warning signs because I didn't want to face the reality of our shitty relationship. He wasn't even good enough at fucking to justify staying with him."

His comment caused me to choke on my last bite.

I drank coffee and tried to clear my throat. "That's…"

"Sorry." He apologized, but the corner of his lips turned upward in a smug grin. "It's true, though. I realized a lot of things like that in your shower this morning."

An image of Xander naked and erect in my shower flashed in my mind. He was gorgeous with his head tilted back as he ran his fingers through his wet hair, the water sluicing down his fit body. I was unprepared for being assailed by the powerful surge of desire that crashed into me hard. What was going on with me? My voice sounded strained as I asked, "Any other revelations you care to share?"

"No, they're naughty enough that I'll keep them to myself, thanks."

My jaw dropped at his teasing. "Come on, you can't say that and not expect me to want examples."

"If you can't figure it out from that context, you should have a second cup of coffee."

More coffee sounded like a splendid idea, minus the part where I was still semi-erect from picturing him in my shower. My pajamas would do nothing to hide that fact. "Are you saying what I think you're saying?"

"That depends. What do you think I'm saying?"

The hormonal side of my brain responsible for my current state of arousal whispered, *That we should fuck.* But I refused to say that out loud. Instead, I played the game with him. "I think you're saying something I want to hear."

"And what would that be?"

Rather than coming up with a clever answer, I told the truth. "Something I never thought you would say."

"Which is?"

I felt like we were playing a game of Questions like we used to when we were kids. It was one of his favorite distraction tactics to get out of talking about something he found uncomfortable. "Why don't you tell me, and I'll let you know if you're right?"

"Why won't you tell me?"

I repeated with emphasis, "Why won't *you* tell *me*?"

"Why do you want to know?" His broad grin betrayed how much fun he was having riling me up.

"Why would you bring it up if you didn't want to tell me?"

"What if I'm just doing this to torture you?"

I knew better than to believe that. "Why are you avoiding telling me by playing a Questions game?"

"Do you really think I have an answer?"

"Would you be playing this game if you didn't?"

Rather than answering, he pivoted. "What if you don't like what I have to say?"

We were finally getting somewhere. "What makes you think I won't like it?"

"Why would you?"

"Why wouldn't I?"

He shrugged. "What am I supposed to do if you hate me for it?"

"Do you think there is anything in this world that could make me hate you?"

"No," he answered with quiet certainty.

I reveled in my victory. "Ha! I win, which means you have to stop playing games and tell me."

"You haven't figured it out yet?"

"Uh-uh, we're not going for the best two out of three," I warned. "I won fair and square. Fess up now, or I get to come up with a punishment game."

"With as many people who have said things to you about me over the years, you've never thought about it?"

I narrowed my eyes at him. "Xander."

He twisted the coffee cup in his hands, not quite able to look at me. "If we're going to get accused of being together anyway, why not enjoy ourselves?"

My heart stuttered in my chest with shock. He couldn't be serious, could he? "Are you asking to be my boyfriend?"

"No, I'm not ready for another relationship." I ignored the painful kick to my gut at his words. "But maybe—I mean, we've both always been willing to do anything for each other because we're best friends, so…"

His implied suggestion filled me with a jumbling mix of confusing reactions, but I wouldn't be satisfied until I heard him clearly state it. "So?"

"So…what if we maybe took things a step further by being friends-with-benefits?" He looked up at me with guarded hope, setting off a chaotic explosion in me at the possibility of what was being offered. "You've been single for a while, and I don't want to mess around with people on dating apps. I trust you more than anyone else in the world, and I know I'm safe with you. Unlike Josh, you'd make sure I enjoyed myself."

Part of me was all too eager to agree, but I had to know something first. "What brought this up?"

A charming blush graced his cheeks as he glanced away in embarrassment. "Because I woke up hard as hell this morning, desperate for a good fuck. But instead, I got in the shower to take care of myself, which wasn't nearly as satisfying. Once I could think again, the experience made me wonder why shouldn't we enjoy each other? It's not like it's the first time the idea has crossed my mind."

His words turned my semi into a full-blown hard-on. But the part that tripped me up the most was the last thing he said. "What do you mean it's not the first time?"

"Remember the New Year's party we went to where I met Josh?"

Not only did I remember, but I had spent *years* trying to forget it without success. We both had too much to drink and crashed as soon as we got home.

But during the night, Xander had somehow found his way into my bed. I had still been drunk enough to think it was a dream, so we made out as I jerked him off. It was only after he came that I realized it had all been real. The incident had been mortifying and forced me to confront feelings I didn't want to deal with. When he pretended like nothing happened, I was all too happy to follow his lead. He started dating Josh almost immediately afterward, so we never brought it up again. "Yes, despite my best efforts to forget."

"I was a little freaked-out at first by how much I liked it. But the more I thought about it, being friends-with-benefits after we had both been single for so long made sense. When I ended up with Josh the weekend afterward and things turned serious between us, I lost my chance."

If I hadn't hated Josh before, I *really* hated him even more now. But I could be bitter later. I had something more important to focus on at the moment. "You seriously want to hook up?"

"If I'm being honest, I'm dying for you to rail me into the mattress so hard I don't want to move until I have to go to work Monday." Shit, if he kept talking like that, I would make a mess out of this pair of underwear, too. "You know, if you're interested." He shrugged, like it was no big deal.

"Oh, I'm interested." My dick standing at full salute was living proof of that. I got up, ready to capitalize on the chance to do what I had dreamed of last night and so many nights before that.

His green-hazel eyes went wide when he saw the evidence of just how into his proposal I was. As soon as he got out of his chair, I scooped him into a cradle hold. He yelped in surprise as he looped his arms around my neck to grab on to me. "Wow, I guess you were paying more attention to those firemen coming to our dorms than I thought."

I chuckled at his jab as I carried him back to my bedroom, eager to give him what we both wanted. There was no point in second-guessing myself with such a golden opportunity presenting itself. I could worry about the potential consequences for my heart after I had satiated my lust.

Chapter Three

XANDER

AS SOON AS Jules put me down in his bedroom, I used his T-shirt to yank him closer and kiss him. I wasn't after tender worship; I wanted something aggressive and dominating that would turn me into a satisfied puddle when we finished. He seemed to get the message as he cupped my face in his hands and took everything from me I was willing to give. His teasing tongue made me weak in the knees, and I clung to him to stay upright.

The passionate kiss filled me with fire, and I fumbled with the zipper as I stripped off the hoodie I had borrowed from him. I never wore them, but I loved stealing his. There was something comforting about being wrapped up in his scent as his clothes hugged me like he did so often. But I didn't want to be consoled right now; I wanted us to be naked.

I pushed up the hem of his aqua T-shirt until he

pulled it off. When we were both bare-chested, I embraced him. His rigid length pressed against my belly, making me ache to feel it inside me. That need intensified as he trailed his fingers down the curve of my spine, before cupping my ass with both of his palms to squeeze it. An involuntary "Fuck yes" escaped from me, causing him to chuckle. "You know, that would feel a lot better if you did it when I wasn't wearing anything."

Not wasting another second, he slid the pajama pants off my hips, letting them fall to the floor. He studied my black trunk-style underwear with neon green trim, which did nothing to hide my bulging erection.

His inaction annoyed me. "Is there some reason you're staring and not touching?"

"Because I had a dream last night. You told me cuddling wasn't the only thing you missed and stripped as a clue."

I laughed at how very me that scenario was. "Either you know me too well, or I'm too predictable."

"You had on a bright purple jockstrap, with neon pink straps that showed off your beautiful ass." He traced the path of where the bands were in his dream, further arousing me. "It was too much temptation to resist."

"Is that your way of saying my trunks aren't doing it for you?"

"No, they're a different kind of sexy." It was a relief when he removed them, leaving me fully nude in front of him. "And for the record, you seduced me, not your underwear."

I returned the favor by stripping him of his pajama pants and briefs. "I'm glad you find me more seductive than cotton—"

He interrupted me with a fierce kiss that I moaned into as he backed us up toward his bed. I fell onto it with a bounce, putting me at eye level with his impressive cock. After six years of mediocre sex, I was desperate for a good dick-down. I regretted all over again not being brave enough to suggest hooking up with Jules when I had the chance. Maybe if I had, I wouldn't have ended up miserable with Josh.

Jules lowered himself to his knees on the floor, nudging my legs apart so he could situate himself between them. Eager for what he was offering, I shifted closer to the edge of the bed and braced my arms backward to give him better access. He held the base of my cock and concentrated on the tip, swirling his tongue around my crown before sucking on it. I clenched the sheets in my hands as he bobbed to take more of me in each time. He made it halfway down my dick before he backed off and focused on the head again. I jerked my hips to slide deeper into his slick heat in search of a more substantial feeling.

My punishment was him backing off to switch his attention to my balls. He sucked one into his mouth to tease it. While it was great, it wasn't what I was after. "Damn it, Julian!"

He sounded far too amused when he asked, "Impatient much?" When he switched to the opposite side, I groaned as it built up my needs that weren't being met.

"Stop being a cocktease!"

"But it's fun getting you riled up." He continued torturing me by running his tongue along the underside of my hardness and then teasing my slit. The slow way he jerked me off in the process did nothing to ease my desperate need to get off.

Since ordering him hadn't worked, I tried a different tactic. "Please, Julie, it's been so long."

"Not as long as it has been for me."

"Then why don't you make us both feel better?"

Instead of answering with words, Jules took me deep into his mouth. I shouted as he vigorously sucked me off like a talented porn star, his nose touching my close-cut pubes as he drank all of me down to the base. His throat worked me as he swallowed, making me lose my damn mind. I scrambled for a hold in his hair as I raced toward my climax. When he slid down my length with his tongue caressing me, I came with a groan of relief. Unlike Josh, Jules licked his lips without complaint to make sure he caught every drop.

My intense release had been amazing, but he was only getting started. He gestured for me to move back on the bed as he grabbed a bottle of lube and a condom. I knelt on all fours, my anticipation building as he got behind me. Rather than his lubed fingers pressing at my entrance that I expected, I gasped when he used his tongue instead. He flicked it against my hole, before spreading me open and dipping it inside me. "Holy *fuck*!" I couldn't even remember the last time I had been so thoroughly pleasured.

Jules was merciless as he teased me with his talented tongue, before stretching me with lubed fingers. I was torn between enjoying the buildup and demanding he move on to better things. It was too much to bear. "I'm good, so *please*!"

I whimpered when he moved away, feeling like I would go out of my mind with lust if I didn't get some relief soon. He tore open the foil packet and put on the condom, before sliding his sheathed cock between my ass cheeks to toy with me. "Julian, I swear to god, if you don't hurry up and fuck me hard, I'll—"

He pushed into me without warning, not stopping until he had bottomed out. I shouted in satisfaction as he gripped my hips and gave me the pounding I desperately desired. He was relentless as he targeted my pleasure point, hitting that spot within me that caused me to shout. I writhed in ecstasy as he took me hard and fast, barely able to breathe because it was so good. "*Yes*!"

Part of me had worried that Jules would be too gentle with me to give me the deep-dicking I needed after years of shitty sex. But to my great surprise and satisfaction, he gave me an aggressive fuck of someone who would never see me again. I didn't expect him to thread his fingers through my hair and hold me down as he plowed me, but I loved every second. His maroon comforter muffled my cries as my body reacted to the roughness by rutting against him with equal force. I couldn't get enough of the ways his balls tapped against mine and the slick sound of our bodies connecting as we worked up a sweat. The experience caused my arousal to return, and I reached down to touch myself for some relief.

In response, Jules's grip in my hair tightened almost to the point of pain, then yanked me up against him as he kept slamming into me. It turned me on even more. "Let me hear your beautiful voice." He nipped at my ear, and I cried out from the sharp burst of pleasure the hurt brought me. "Louder."

When I didn't react immediately, he shoved me face-first onto the bed. He slowed his pace and switched to shallow thrusts, which was the exact opposite of what I craved. "Please, Julie! Fuck me, damn it!"

He obliged me, resuming his earlier harsher rhythm as he pushed in as deep as he could go. I was in heaven until he repositioned us by resting on his haunches and guiding me up to lean against him. My irritation subsided when I realized the change allowed me more freedom to bounce as roughly as I wanted to. He made it even better when he wrapped his hand around my renewed hardness and started jerking me off. I reached behind and buried my fingers in his damp blond hair, tilting my head with a whimper as I tensed up in anticipation of another release. All I needed was a little more to take me over the edge. Him licking up my neck to tug on my earlobe with his teeth did it for me.

My second orgasm hit me hard, taking Jules with me as he came after a few more thrusts. I sagged against him, overwhelmed by the experience. Every molecule inside of me sang in glory from the dizzying heights of sexual gratification I felt down to my bones. He hugged me, moaning next to my ear as he nuzzled me. We remained in our intimate embrace, still panting from the aggressive fucking. It had been exactly what I needed, and I was so grateful to my best friend for being willing to give me what I wanted most and then some.

I trembled from the overwhelming exertion. Jules guided me to lie down, pulling out of me as I collapsed onto the comforter with a satisfied groan. I expected him to curl up with me, but he went into his bathroom and returned with a warm washcloth. The gentle way he cleaned me made me feel a bit choked up. Aftercare was a nonexistent concept to Josh, so Jules's tenderness overwhelmed me while not at all surprising. That was just who he was. I couldn't help but be jealous of all his ex-boyfriends who probably hadn't appreciated that about him.

After he finished, he pulled the sheets out from under me and covered us up as he joined me in bed. Like I had the previous night, I draped myself on top of him as he snuggled with me. It was even better this time because we were both naked and exhausted from the best sex I had ever had. He caressed my back, sending little aftershocks of pleasure skittering through me. It was a stark contrast to Josh rolling over and going to sleep immediately after we finished. Damn, I was such an idiot for not doing this with my best friend sooner.

Jules interrupted my afterglow to ask in a worried tone, "Was I too rough?"

Without thought, I kissed his shoulder to reassure him. "No, that was *perfect*. It was everything I needed and then some." He held me tighter, and I nuzzled against him with a contented sigh. The comforting thrum of his heartbeat relaxed me further. "When I'm capable of feeling something other than euphoria, I'll kick myself later for choosing Josh over you. He wasn't worth missing out on the best sex of my life."

"I thought you said your ex-boyfriend Apollo was your ultimate sex god?"

"Congratulations, you've demoted him to demigod status." I grinned as Jules burst into laughter. "It makes sense when you think about it. You're closer to me than anyone, so you know what I need before I do a lot of times. It doesn't surprise me that carries over to satisfying me in the bedroom. But instead of enjoying this, I went with the schmuck who barely knows the difference between an asshole and a hole in the ground."

"Your poor ass." He laughed as one of his hands snuck down for a consoling grope. "I promise I'll take better care of you."

Snuggling against him, I was boneless and at ease as I replied, "You always do."

"And I always will."

Adrift in the satisfaction of my back-to-back orgasms and the warm glow of our friendship, I soon drifted to sleep in my best friend's arms. It was the happiest and most satisfied I had ever been in my life.

I WOKE up with Jules curled around me, hugging me close to him. Even unconscious, he embraced me with his everything. It was strange for me, because Josh had never once sought me out in his sleep. He always stayed on the far side of the bed, wanting nothing to do with me unless it involved fucking. I had convinced myself I was fine with that, but my morning romp had forced me to realize how wrong I had been.

It wasn't that I didn't need physical closeness; I just never felt like I required it from Josh. Whenever I craved a connection with someone to reassure myself,

I always sought out Jules. He was the only one who knew how to make me feel better, no matter what happened. A single hug from him made all my problems disappear, even the catastrophic ones. That was why I never relied on Josh or any of my ex-boyfriends for comfort, because Jules was the sole person capable of giving me that.

I hadn't realized how much I missed being held until that moment. He cradled me as if I was the most precious thing in the world to him. His embrace gave me a sense of peace and security, and a certainty that nothing bad could happen to me while I was in his arms. How long had it been since I felt that way with a boyfriend? It was depressing realizing the answer was maybe never. None of my exes had ever given me that level of comfort, because I hadn't allowed them to get close enough to me to do so. Jules was the only person I let past my barriers, because I knew without a doubt that he would never hurt me. It was no wonder all my romances failed. Why hadn't I made that connection until now?

For someone who was so smart, how could I be so damn dumb? Being satisfied on every level by Jules that morning had shown me what an idiot I was. Why would I think others could give me that kind of pleasure when I couldn't lower my guard around them? It was only with my best friend that I felt safe enough to be myself, to let go completely without worrying about the consequences. That was because I trusted him in a manner no one else had ever proven they deserved. Did that mean all my relationships in the future would fail for the same reason?

"Shhh, keep it down." Jules's voice came out in a deep rumble, making my dick perk up with interest. "I can hear you thinking."

"About what?"

His answer shouldn't have surprised me. "You're overthinking what it means that I made you feel better than your asshole exes."

When we were kids, Jules used to pretend that he was psychic and could read my mind. While I logically knew that was impossible, sometimes he would be so accurate that I almost had to wonder. "What was my conclusion?"

He yawned before replying. "You trust me enough to be yourself. There's nothing wrong with that, so stop worrying."

I rolled over to face him with a frown. "If I couldn't be myself with Josh after six years of being together, why the hell did I waste so much time with him?" The unspoken *instead of being with you* hung heavy between us.

Jules reached out and pulled me into another hug. "Don't focus on that."

"But it's not just Josh! All of my exes—"

He stopped me with a soft but insistent kiss. I was quickly becoming a big fan of his silencing technique.

"You're spiraling. There's no need to beat yourself up for stuff in the past. It changes nothing."

"But what about the future?"

"Does worrying about it now help?"

How could I not be concerned about it? In what future would I find a man who could make me feel as good as Jules did? Who understood me the same way? Where was I supposed to meet this mythical person who didn't exist? And what did that mean about our friends-with-benefits arrangement? Would it go on indefinitely, or was there an end date for when it was all over? What if that deadline was when Jules found someone he wanted to be with more?

Acid churned in my stomach at that unbearable thought. It drove me to act without thinking, pushing Jules onto his back to straddle myself over him. Before he could ask a question, I kissed him hard, demanding entrance to his mouth with my tongue. He opened for me, letting me explore him with a passionate need for more. He was right; the future didn't matter when he was mine for now.

Kiss melted into kiss, his hands heightening my pleasure as they caressed along my back and sides. It left me hard and wanting, but I wasn't the only one. I rocked against him, brushing our erections together with pleasing results. It spurred me to brace my arms on either side of Jules's head as I started rubbing my dick against his while we made out. He grabbed my ass to help guide my hips as I rutted against him like a horny teenager who couldn't slow down long enough for a proper fuck. My desire for him was too intense to stop.

When he took both of our cocks in hand to jerk us off at the same time, I keened with desperation. Like a man possessed, I chased the sensations with my insatiable lust. As suddenly as I had started, I moaned as I came. He followed suit, our cum mixing on his stomach.

I may have gotten off, but that didn't lessen my need for my best friend. Not wanting to think anymore, I kept kissing him until I forgot about my problems. Anything was better than dealing with the uncomfortable realization that maybe no one else would ever satisfy me as much as Jules did.

AFTER LUNCH, Jules and I watched a movie in his living room. I stretched out on the couch, resting my head in his lap. He stroked my hair like a pet, and it soothed me in ways I hadn't known were possible. But those obnoxious regrets from before continued bubbling in the back of my mind, encroaching on my comfort.

I hadn't even noticed he paused the movie until he asked, "What's wrong?"

With effort, I shifted to look up at him. "With what?"

He rubbed away the furrow in my brow, drawing my attention to my pinched expression. "With you."

I said nothing as he traced the delicate arch of one of my eyebrows with the pad of his thumb. When we were teens, he had once been forced into confessing during a game of truth or dare that he that found my "elegant eyebrows" attractive. He had taken a lot of shit about it from our friends, but the compliment had always stuck in the back of my brain. As he reverently brushed over my other one, I had to ask. "How long have you wanted to do that?"

"Answer my question first, and I'll consider telling you."

Left with no choice but to admit what was bothering me, I told the truth. "I realized how long it's been since we've spent the whole day hanging out together like this, because Josh always lost his shit when we did. Instead of telling him to pack his bags and get out, I took the coward's way out and stopped spending as much time with you as I wanted to. It was easier than fighting with him about it." Regret ate away at me. "I'm the worst."

"No, you're not." He caressed the ridge of my cheekbone to comfort me. "You did what you had to do."

"I don't know what I was thinking. Why was I willing to give up my time with you, when you're the one who makes me happiest, to spend it with him, who made me miserable?"

"Because you knew that no matter what, I'd still be waiting for you when it was over."

The truth behind his words sickened me. He was right. I had been able to spend less time with him, because I knew he would never hold it against me the way Josh would if the situation was reversed. When shit went down, Jules would always take me back without complaint, no matter how much I ignored him while I was with my partner. It had been that way since my first boyfriend. "I—"

He put his finger over my lips to shush me. "I didn't say that to make you feel bad. You don't have to apologize for wanting to spend more time with your boyfriend. That's not a problem; it's how it's supposed to be."

I sat up and straddled myself over his lap, allowing me to throw my arms around him and hide my face against his neck. He hugged me tight, overwhelming me with a rush of messy feelings I was too upset to sort through. "I'm so sorry, Julie."

He rubbed my upper back in consolation. "You have nothing to be sorry about."

I appreciated him being willing to absolve me of my guilt so easily, but I didn't deserve it. "No, I'm sorry that I picked him, that I've wasted the last six years of my life with him at the expense of our friendship, and—"

"Stop beating yourself up, Xander. It's not worth it. Our friendship is stronger than ever, and you gain nothing by making yourself feel bad about something I'm not mad at you about."

I pulled back with a frown to look at him. "But you should be upset with me for it!"

He cupped my face in his palms as he gazed at me with so much affection it stole my breath away. "How can I be upset when I'm the one holding you right now and not him?"

Leaning forward, I kissed him with the full force of my jumbled emotions. Like always, he was the only thing capable of alleviating the tumultuous chaos inside me. I had made so many wrong decisions in my past, but as I claimed his lips as mine, I knew without a doubt that I had finally made the right one.

Chapter Four

JULES

I HAD FUCKED MORE in the past two days than I had in the last four years combined. It was as if now that we didn't need to hold back anymore, Xander and I were desperately trying to make up for lost time. We went at it like rabbits who couldn't get enough of each other. I had lost track of how many times we had done it. Whenever I thought I had nothing left in me, he would give me a certain look and my cock rediscovered its will to live again. And if that didn't work, he had found great success in commanding me, "Get hard, damn it!" God, I loved it when he got authoritative with me. So did my dick.

But this time, I was well and truly tapped out as I held Xander in my arms. He had collapsed on top of me and stayed there, too satiated to move. The weight of him reassured me what was happening between us was very real. It wasn't another dream of mine that I would be forced to ignore for the sake of my own sanity. Reality turned out to be so much more gratifying than even my best dreams. It also proved my imagination was severely limited, because I never dreamed about enjoying an all-out fuckfest like we had indulged in since Saturday. I couldn't imagine being so lucky.

After coming so many times, I was down to my last brain cell. Because of that, I allowed myself to cradle Xander against me as if he was my most precious person. I was too exhausted to remember that he wasn't really mine, and it was wrong to never want to let him go again. There wasn't enough energy left in me to fend off the realization that while the sex was amazing, holding him after we came was the ultimate pleasure for me.

Cuddling had always been one of my favorite kinds of hugging, but it was different with Xander. It felt like we had somehow merged our souls together to form an unbreakable bond between us. Embracing him made me feel complete, because he was the other half of me. They were thoughts I *really* shouldn't have about my best friend and new fuck buddy.

But when I held him, it also comforted me, especially after aggressively pleasuring Xander. I enjoyed the occasional tear each other's clothes off and fuck on the floor because you couldn't make it to the bed kind of sex. And more than anything, I loved giving my partner whatever they desired with no judgment. But sometimes I worried I went too far.

It was fine he indulged in some pain to enhance his pleasure, but I was uncomfortable with the prospect of doing actual damage to his body. I trusted him to know his limits, but I understood how easy it would be for him to go overboard now that his pent-up needs could finally be met.

That's why holding him afterward comforted me that I hadn't harmed him. It was a way for me to apologize for getting too rough, even though he had begged and pleaded for more the entire time. I wondered if once he got all the aggression out of his system if I'd ever be allowed to indulge him with some tenderness.

As much as I wanted that, the prospect troubled me. If I was gentle, if I reverently worshipped him, if I cherished him the way I secretly wished to, that line between friendship and love would get dangerously blurred. Snuggling with him was already risky enough when it made me feel like I needed nothing else in the world as long as I could hold him.

"Mmfph."

Xander's soft noise pulled me from my thoughts. "Hmm?"

"Nngh."

I wasn't sure what either of those translated to, other than I had sexually satisfied him to the point where he forgot the entire English language. That was a nice stroke to the ego. "Mm?"

He was silent for a moment, before an "unf" escaped from him.

Our nonverbal conversation amused me. "Mmm."

He groaned in protest, still not quite up to words yet.

Instead of continuing the game, I hazarded a guess at what he was trying to say. "Does that translate to you need to go, but you don't want to move?"

"Mm-hmm."

I caressed his back, sending a shiver through him. "I don't have anywhere to be until dinner with my brother tonight. It's fine if you stay a little longer." I wasn't in any hurry to leave. If I had my way, I'd hold him for the rest of time.

He sighed heavily as he nuzzled against my shoulder with a pouty "Work." It was so damn cute to see him in such a rare state.

Since he had come over to my place Friday night on an impulse, he hadn't brought his laptop to take care of things. It was no wonder the workaholic inside of him was going nuts. I was sympathetic, but also very pleased that I had worn him out enough that he didn't want to go. "Do you need me to help you get up?"

"Can't. All fucked out."

I laughed, causing him to harrumph. "Well, you *did* say you wished I'd rail you into the mattress so hard you didn't want to move until you had to go to work Monday. You know how much I love a good challenge."

"Ugh, I don't want to move for like a month of Mondays."

"Ooh, I finally got a full sentence."

My comment earned me a deserved pinch to the side that caused me to startle. "Smart-ass."

It was impossible to resist getting a little payback by reaching down to give his a squeeze. "Perfect-ass." When I dipped my fingers between his cheeks, he automatically rocked back against me.

He groaned, *"Don't,"* but it came out more of a wanton plea than an objection. "Seriously, I won't survive."

"You've said that the last three times, but miraculously found a way each time." I trailed my fingertips up the curve of his spine, raising chills on his pale skin. "Are you sure?"

"I don't have the energy to roll off of you, and you think I can withstand another onslaught of pleasure?"

He shuddered when I chuckled. "That sounds like a challenge to me."

"Julian."

"Xander." When he whimpered in distress, I moved my wandering hand up to stroke his brown hair. "Relax, I'm only teasing you."

"If I get any more relaxed, I'll be dead."

I laughed again. "Well, we can't have that now, can we?"

"Preferably not."

"Let me rephrase my original question: Do you need me to help get you out of bed?"

Xander toyed with my hair. "I need to say yes, but I also kind of want to stay right here forever. Maybe take a nap."

"Forever sounds good." It was only after the words had escaped that I realized that was a comment best left unexpressed in my skull. Oops.

He fell silent, but I knew he hadn't fallen asleep because he was still petting the nape of my neck. It could have been two minutes or two hours before he asked, "Why did we resist this for so long?"

"Probably because I'm a contrarian asshole who dug himself deeper into denial every time someone told me I had a crush on you." Damn, that answer was a little more honest than I had been prepared to share.

"Meaning the more people told you that you liked me, the more you had to prove to them you didn't?"

I shrugged. "What can I say? My brother's the genius, not me."

He sounded sad when he asked, "I guess I was basically doing the same thing, huh?"

I hugged him tighter, not wanting to dwell on something that depressing when I was happy he was in my arms. "We don't have to think about that now."

"Okay."

He fell asleep quickly after that, but I stayed awake for a while. If I only had a limited time to enjoy our arrangement, I needed to memorize every second to keep me company when it was over. No matter how much I wished it were possible, forever wasn't an option.

AFTER XANDER LEFT my apartment on Sunday night, I headed over to my younger brother's place for dinner. It gave me time to decompress after spending two days of non-stop enjoyment of my new friends-with-benefits arrangement. Deep down, I was aware of how dangerous it was, because the odds of me losing my heart to him were bad. But the sex had been the most satisfying of my life, so I hit the snooze button on my concerns to deal with later.

It was much easier to focus on the delicious bourbon-chocolate mousse Rune had prepared for dessert. "Wow, even by your standards, this is incredible."

"For an experiment, it turned out pretty good." Dressed in a white sweater with the sleeves pushed up and a pair of black jeans, he effortlessly made it high fashion. As a model, it was his job to make things look great, and he did it so well he was rightfully famous for it. I was handsome, but my brother was blessed with beauty on an extraordinary level. With his icy blue eyes, dark hair, chiseled features, and enigmatic charm, it was obvious why he had such a successful career.

"Callum will love this when he gets home." That was an understatement. He was an enormous fan of all things dessert.

The mere mention of his boyfriend made Rune smile. It was adorable seeing him so in love after spending most of his life alone and miserable. "I hope so."

I savored another bite of the creamy mousse. "Can you give this recipe to Xander? He'd enjoy this, too." It also meant I could bug him to make it and not just my younger brother, doubling my odds of enjoying it again in the future.

"Sure." Rune studied me, like he was trying to solve a great mystery.

"What?"

"Something's different about you tonight."

I had to remind my paranoia it wasn't possible for him to tell I had gotten laid right before coming over. "Not really."

He continued looking at me for some kind of clue. "You're the most relaxed I've seen you in years. You mentioned earlier that Xander made you breakfast this weekend. He broke up with his boyfriend last week. Putting all those pieces together, am I wrong to believe you two finally did something about your feelings for each other?"

My little brother was too smart for his own good. "Nothing happened regarding our feelings, because we don't have any for each other like that."

He scoffed the same way he had every other time I had insisted that was true. "Bullshit. You're sidestepping the issue, which tells me I'm closer to being right than you're comfortable with."

"Does it?" I scraped the bottom of the shallow white bowl he served the mousse in that had some fancy technical name I didn't know.

Rune refused to relent. "I've known Xander since I was five, so that's, what, almost twenty-six years of him being your best friend? He's one of the most logical people I've ever met. He's single now, and you've been alone for ages. After being in a shitty relationship for so long, he's probably in the mood to enjoy himself to the fullest but doesn't have the patience for idiots on dating apps. If that doesn't spell out a perfect friends-with-benefits scenario between you two, I'm not sure what does."

I huffed in annoyance. Damn him for being so perceptive. "Aren't you cute playing detective? Trying out another potential career?"

He smirked. "I know I'm right."

"Fine, you're right. So what?"

His smug satisfaction morphed into concern. Damn it, that was even worse. "So, what are you going to do about it?"

"Enjoy getting laid after an embarrassingly long dry spell and not think two thoughts about it."

"Do you seriously expect you can do that without falling deeper in love with him?"

I crossed my arms over my chest with a glare. "Yes, because I'm not in love with him at all."

"Uh-huh. Sure."

"I'm not!" I sounded petulant, but I didn't care. Just because I was older by three years didn't mean I always had to act like it.

He took a sip of water as he continued staring me down. "Protest all you want, but being with him will dredge up all those feelings you've been cramming down for over twenty years, trying to pretend they don't exist."

His words touched on a genuine fear of mine, but I shrugged it off. "Whatever. It's just sex."

"For someone who lies to himself all the time about being in love with his best friend, you're terrible at it."

"I'm not lying!" It was a total coincidence it was the greatest and most fulfilling sex of my life. That didn't mean I was in love with Xander.

Rune's arctic gaze softened as he looked at me with concern. "What's wrong with using this opportunity to be honest with yourselves? It's not as if it's all one-sided on your end."

"If Xander wanted to be with me, he wouldn't have spent the last six years of his life dating that asshole. He would have stayed with me in our apartment together. But he made his choice, and he hasn't changed his mind, even with Josh out of the picture." Everything I said was true, and I hated that it hurt me on some level. It shouldn't feel like a stiletto heel kick to the balls, but it did. *Damn it.*

"Did it ever occur to you that Xander suggested your arrangement as a way of easing you both into an actual relationship?"

My initial reaction was a very inappropriate hope that I forced myself to ignore. "What makes you think it's his idea?"

Rune gave me a look that told me exactly how stupid he thought my question was. "Because I know both of you too well. You've always let him take the lead with you two, because you understand he needs that level of control to be comfortable. Now, whether he's aware of that is an entirely different story."

"It sounds manipulative when you put it that way." I frowned at the idea. "You're also giving me far too much credit when a lot of it comes down to the only thing I care about is if he's happy. He enjoys being the one in command, and I'm cool going with the flow because I implicitly trust him with everything."

"And that doesn't sound like love to you?"

I nudged the empty dish across the table with my spoon. "That's just being a good friend."

My brother tried another angle. "What's so wrong with being in love with him?"

"Because he said he doesn't want a boyfriend. It would be a mistake for me to assume he's after anything other than a fun time. I'm not willing to push for more, because—"

When I cut myself off, he finished my sentence. "Because you're too scared you'll lose him."

That was exactly what I was going to say, and I didn't like hearing it out of his mouth any more than mine. It put me on the defensive. "Why the hell are you trying to psychoanalyze me, anyway? Are you planning on going back to school for a PhD in psychology now?"

"I don't need a degree in psychology to understand you're doing Olympic-level mental gymnastics to keep yourself from admitting you're in love with him and have been for years."

"Even if that *was* true, he just got out of a six-year relationship. I'm not interested in being his rebound. He's entitled to have some fun now that he's single, and if that's with me, great. At least that way I don't have to worry about some asshole hurting him."

"If you don't think Xander will figure out he's having all of his physical and emotional needs met by you, you don't understand him nearly as well as you think."

I bristled at the implication. "I know him plenty well, thanks."

"Then you should also know he'll do the math soon and conclude that being with you is the only solution that makes sense. Why don't you make it easier for him by finally being honest about what you really want?"

I didn't have an answer to that question. Thankfully, Callum entering the apartment spared me. He had beautiful auburn hair, deep blue eyes, and was so cute that it was easy to see why Rune had fallen head over heels in love with him. He looked adorable as always in one of his stylish bow ties as he walked over to the dining area. My brother had indulged his boyfriend's interest in them. I could only imagine how many he had added to his collection over the past few months. "Hey, Callum."

"Hi! I was hoping you'd still be here," he said in his beautiful Irish accent. He came over and gave me a hug hello. I appreciated that he was a hugger and had managed the impossible feat of turning Rune into one after a lifetime of despising hugs. "It's been forever since I've seen you. I miss you stopping by at work."

"Sorry, I've been trying to stay out of your office because Xander's slammed with wedding preparations. He needs to focus on that more than me." My brother arched an eyebrow at me in silent judgment. "Hey, don't look at me like that."

Rune ignored me and kissed his boyfriend. "Welcome home, baby. There's some bourbon-chocolate mousse in the fridge for you."

Callum squealed with delight as he threw his arms around him in another hug. "You're the best!" His love for desserts was legendary at this point.

I couldn't resist teasing him a little. "You're lucky I like you so much. It's so good, I wanted to eat yours for seconds."

He laughed as he went into the kitchen to get his treat, then came back to join us at the glass table. His initial reaction didn't disappoint, as he sighed while savoring the first bite. "Oh, this is *amazing*! Brody and Augie would love this!"

"I already sent the recipe to them." It was great that Rune had also become friends with Callum's family. "How were the guys?"

"They're relieved midterms are over and it's spring break. It was nice hanging out with Wren and Izzy again. Felix and North invited me over to their place to have a movie night on Friday, but we'll do it another time since Rhys's wedding is on Saturday. I want to get there early and help Xander if any last-minute issues come up."

Not only was Callum good to my brother, he was a gift to my best friend. "On Xander's behalf, thank you. Hopefully, it'll all go smoothly."

"I think it will, but I'll feel better knowing I'm around if there's a problem."

Rune reached out and stroked Callum's hair. "That's sweet of you."

He blushed under the praise.

Since I was sure my brother wanted to welcome Callum back in other ways after being in Italy for a week on business, I did the gracious thing. "I should head home soon." It also got me out of having a follow-up conversation about what we discussed earlier.

"Aww, really?" Callum asked in disappointment. "Oh, I have an idea! What if you and Xander had dinner with us once the wedding stuff is over? We'll be on vacation for three weeks, so it'll be the perfect time for a nice, relaxing evening."

"I think that sounds like an excellent plan, baby." Rune's expression told me I was in for some meddling in my relationship with Xander if that plan came to fruition.

Ignoring it, I got up and gave Callum a goodbye hug. "I'll see you next weekend at the wedding."

Rune escorted me to the door, so I joked with him, "You know the punishment for coming over here to get in a final smart-ass comment is you're getting hugged, right?"

"Nice try. You would hug me either way." He beat me to it by embracing me first. I never took it for granted considering how much he used to hate physical affection. Callum truly was a miracle worker. "I'll tell you the same thing you told me when I was struggling with my feelings for Callum. You're allowed to want love, Jules. You're allowed to want *him*. You didn't accept any of my protests, because you knew they were bullshit. So, why are you accepting your own?"

"Damn it, why did I have to give you such stellar advice?" I laughed as I pulled back. "Thanks for the awesome dinner tonight. I hope you know how happy I am for you and Callum."

His serene smile told me everything. "I do."

"See? Every once in a while, your older brother knows what he's doing." It was only my situation with Xander I didn't know what the fuck I was trying to accomplish.

"From time to time." He glanced over to the kitchen where Callum was putting away the dishes. "I'll never be able to thank you enough for bringing him into my life. He's my everything, Jules. I know you understand what I mean, because Xander has always been that for you, too."

I wanted to argue, but I couldn't. Not when Xander had been my entire universe since we were eight.

Rune's imploring gaze tugged on my heartstrings. "Please believe me when I say it feels so much better to give in and be happy than to keep running away in fear. You told me I deserved to be with Callum no matter what my inner demons said. Why don't you think that's true about you with Xander?"

I didn't have a good answer to that, so I took the coward's way out. "I'll see you at the wedding on Saturday. Love you."

"Love you, too."

After a few more parting words, I left my brother's apartment to head home. It was annoying having my previous wise words thrown back at me. The real question was, would I listen to my own excellent advice?

Chapter Five

XANDER

IT WAS rare for me to be in such high spirits at the start of the workweek. But after being satisfied all weekend with the best sex of my life, not even a busy Monday could get me down. I could still feel the residual soreness in my muscles from the nonstop pleasure I had enjoyed, compliments of my best friend. The physical reminder kept me on the edge of arousal all day. There was only one thing capable of fucking up my mood, and he just knocked on my open office door. I narrowed my eyes at Josh, who had no reason to visit me when he wasn't part of Rhys's personal team of attorneys.

"Hey, Xander. Got a minute?"

It was only because Rhys was out and Callum was at lunch that I allowed myself to be catty enough to reply, "For you? No."

Instead of taking the hint to leave, Josh entered

my office and shut the door behind him. I bristled as he sat down at the chair across from my desk. He was still annoyingly good-looking, blessed with a handsome face that hid what an ugly asshole he was until it was too late. Because of that, he coasted through life with the arrogant confidence only a mediocre man could possess. He was the kind of bastard who was five nine but told everyone he was six feet tall. The petty part of me reveled in the fact that I actually was six feet tall and he hated that. I never understood why it mattered; it's not like I cared that Jules was four inches taller than me.

"How are you holding up?" I loathed how he asked that question with the fake sympathy of someone who thought they were better than you. It made me want to break his perfect nose. Ugh, what had I ever seen in him in the first place besides a pretty face?

"I'm doing fantastic." Thanks to Jules, that wasn't a lie. "For somebody who used to be so concerned about people thinking we were together, it's awful bold of you to come in here and close the door."

"We have things to discuss that shouldn't be overheard."

"I have nothing to say to you, other than get out."

"There's no need to be like that," he chided me, setting my teeth on edge. "We're perfectly capable of being civil with each other like adults."

With effort, I bit back my angry retort. It was

obvious he was trying to goad me into a fight, but I refused to give him the satisfaction of ruffling my feathers. Instead of cutting him down to size with words like I wanted to do, I did the second-best thing. I gave him the silent treatment, because he *hated* that. Since he was an attorney, he thought he could argue everything, but it was impossible to do that when the other person didn't fight back. He liked the battle, so I took great pleasure in denying him that.

Josh cleared his throat as he shifted in the chair. "Speaking of being civil, I wanted to make sure that there won't be any issues with me bringing my boyfriend to Rhys's wedding this week."

"One, you're not bringing him to the wedding when you're Elias's plus-one. Two, he's not your boyfriend; he's just a willing hole who doesn't know any better than to trust you." Oh well, so much for civility.

"Look, you can be mad at me all you want, but you should still treat Elias with the respect owed to him as my boyfr—"

"*Respect?*" I clenched my jaw as I struggled to rein in my emotions. No, I refused to let Josh win. "It has nothing to do with respect. Elias isn't your boyfriend, no matter what you say. It's obvious to everyone but him that you're using him to con his dad into promoting you to managing counselor now that Jenkins announced her retirement. And quite frankly, Elias deserves better than your bullshit."

Josh had the gall to look scandalized by my assessment of the situation. "I would *never* do that to him!" It was impressive that he had the audacity to pair mock outrage with his faux indignation.

"Why? Because you love him *soooo* much?" I lost the battle against my self-restraint and rolled my eyes at him. "Please, you aren't a talented enough liar to make anyone believe that."

"I'm sorry that I hurt you, but—"

Not interested in hearing more of his nonsense, I cut him off. "Save it. I refuse to listen to you apologize again so you can make yourself feel better about what a piece of shit you are."

"Well, I feel terrible you have to go to Rhys's wedding all alone now." He almost looked remorseful, but I knew better.

"Oh, *that's* what you feel terrible for? Not all the cheating and the lying? Interesting." I took far more pleasure in my next revelation than I should have. "For your information, I'm not going alone. My new boyfriend is joining me." Bless Jules for being willing to go pretend to be my date as part of my payback plan. It would be sweet revenge given how much Josh despised him.

"You have a new boyfriend?" he asked in shock. "Since when?"

I shrugged it off as no big deal. "Did you really expect me to sit at home and cry into ice cream over you?"

"We were together for six years!"

"If that fact didn't stop you from cheating on me, why should it matter now that we're not together anymore?"

Josh looked like I slapped him across the face with my question. Good. "But—"

"You're sorely mistaken if you think I'll waste another second on you. I'm much better off with my new boyfriend who actually makes me happy and knows how to keep me satisfied in *every* way." I let the word "every" drip with all the innuendo I meant to make sure he got the point, before I used his words against him. "Please try to be civil when you meet him at the wedding and treat him with the respect owed to him as my new boyfriend. After all, it's the least you could do after wasting the last six years of my life."

Josh's jaw dropped, and he glared at me with an anger that thrilled me. "He'll *never* treat you like I did!"

"Yes, you're right. He'll treat me better than you ever did, because he loves and respects me enough not to cheat on me. I'm glad you see that now. Good for you, Josh."

He balled his hands into fists, opening and closing his mouth several times to say something, but no words came out.

I gave him a saccharine smile as I told him, "You know, it's funny. I didn't realize that you were what made me so miserable these past few years. I almost owe you a thank-you for the breakup, because it's the best thing that's ever happened to me."

When he stormed off without another word in a fuming rage, I celebrated my victory. Sure, I had been petty as fuck, but it felt *so* good after all the bullshit he put me through. At least with the door shut and everyone around my office gone, nobody had heard the confrontation. I had a reputation at work of being unflappable and always in control of everything. There was no way I'd let that asshole show them I was anything less than perfect. Jules was the only person I allowed to see the imperfect parts of myself I wished weren't there.

Another knock on my door caused me to glance up, and I was grateful it was Callum this time. With his auburn hair, blue eyes, and bright smile, he was a refreshing ray of sunshine in our office. He had on a three-piece gray suit with a lilac plaid bow tie, looking adorable as ever. "I wanted to let you know that I'm back. Is there anything you want me to take care of while you go to lunch?"

For years, I had insisted on working alone because no one's standards were ever as good enough as mine. But Callum continued to be the one exception to that rule. I'd never stop being appreciative that Rhys had hired him to help me. It was rare to have someone who volunteered to do extra work instead of kill time on their phone. "Would you mind pulling the files for the Davros acquisition? I want to start on that next."

"They'll be on your desk when you get back."

"Thank you, Callum."

His cheery smile brightened my mood, which immediately crashed into a fiery grave when he turned around and bumped into the person I least wanted to see after Josh—Elias. Paperwork went flying as the two young men apologized to each other and crouched down to pick up everything on the floor. I watched with apathetic eyes as I steeled myself for whatever was about to happen.

When Elias stood up, he clutched his papers as he adjusted his rimless glasses and looked everywhere but at me. "Um, I'm sorry for the interruption, Xander, but if you have a moment, I'd like to talk to you about—"

I gestured for him to come in and told Callum, "If you could shut the door behind you, I'd appreciate it."

"Will do." Callum did as I requested, the sound of it closing making Elias startle. He had always been on the quieter side, but the jumpiness was new. It made me suspect Josh had been telling him all kinds of awful stories about me.

As I had with my ex, I let the silence drag out into an uncomfortable moment that unnerved him further. His slight build made him seem smaller than he was, which I was sure was another reason Josh had targeted him. Elias had delicate features, white-blond hair, and gentle gray eyes. Someone as gorgeous as him who was a corporate attorney should've had an ego the size of Texas. Somehow, he was humble and soft-spoken, shy to an almost painful degree. It bothered me he had probably only consented to Josh because he didn't know how to stand up to somebody as forceful as him.

His voice was barely louder than a whisper as he apologized. "I'm sorry to bother you, but Josh asked me to bring you this for Rhys's signature."

Of course he did. I gritted my teeth as my annoyance flared over the intentional subterfuge on Josh's part. I held my hand out to accept the documents, then signaled him to sit. After he complied, I skimmed through what he had given me. It was paperwork from a deal finished two years ago that already had Rhys's signature on it. Josh had clearly sent Elias on a fool's errand purely to rub him in my face. *That fucking bastard.*

I pinned Elias under my gaze, who shrunk back into his chair. "Did you look at this?"

"No, but he said it was important that I brought it to you at one o'clock." Right, because that wasn't suspicious at all.

"And you didn't find it the least bit strange that someone who isn't part of Rhys's legal team was asking you to get his signature? Especially during the week he's out of the office to prepare for his wedding?"

He fidgeted with his glasses again, not quite able to meet my gaze. "Admittedly, it seemed odd, but if he asked me to do it, then I assumed there had to be a reason."

I tossed the document onto my desk in front of him, causing him to wince as it hit the wood. "Why don't you flip through this and tell me one good reason you can think of that he would ask you to bring this over here in person?"

Obedient to a fault, Elias picked up the papers with trembling fingers and reviewed everything. His narrow eyebrows furrowed as he discovered the same thing I did. "Wait, this doesn't make any sense. This is a closed deal Rhys already signed off on two years ago. Sorry, he must have made a mistake and given me the wrong paperwork, or—"

"It wasn't a mistake. He did this deliberately."

Elias looked up at me in confusion. "What do you mean?"

In that moment, I realized how young and naïve he was at twenty-five. He reminded me of Callum in the sense that they both were such pure souls who didn't know how to see the bad in somebody. Callum lucked out and fell in love with Rune, who thought he was the sun, the moon, and the stars. Poor Elias got stuck with manipulative Josh, who saw him as nothing more than a means to an end to get what he wanted. I couldn't help but pity him. It irritated me Josh would use someone as kind as Elias as a pawn to upset me over his flagrant indiscretion.

The spurned part of my heart almost wanted to let Elias find out for himself how awful Josh was. However, the thought of my ex-boyfriend ruining the next six years of his life with lies and misery didn't sit well with me. I liked him too much not to at least try to open his eyes a little. "Let me guess: Josh told you I broke his heart by leaving him, didn't he? I bet he insisted you would never hurt him like that because you're so kind." Elias stiffened at my words. "You probably never went to his place, because something was always wrong with it, right? And that's why he had to move in with you last week, plus he was tired of having to say goodbye to you?"

"How did you know that?" He trembled as he stared at me with confused gray eyes.

"Because that's the same bullshit he told me six years ago about his previous boyfriend so I'd let him move in with me a few months after we met." I was an idiot for only connecting the dots now. "Since I evicted him last week, I had a feeling he'd use that line again on you."

Tears welled up in Elias's eyes. "But he said you left him months ago for your best friend. He told me the two of you were never serious, which is why no one knew you were dating."

My rage spiked that he blamed Jules, before it turned into a pleased purr. Our plan to be fake boyfriends at the wedding was sure to drive Josh nuts. "No, we lived together as boyfriends for six years. When I found out about the cheating last week, I kicked him out of my apartment."

Elias looked like he would be sick. He couldn't hold back his tears as he stumbled while getting up to leave. "I'm so sorry, I can't be here." With those words, he rushed out of my office with the old documents still clutched in his hands.

It was a hollow victory. Nothing felt good about making Elias cry over the realization he was dating a cheating asshole. He was just a kid who didn't have a clue about what Josh was really like. I had been twenty-eight when I met Josh and I hadn't known any better, either. Maybe it was too much to hope for that Elias would take the warning to heart and leave Josh. But at least I had said something instead of letting him continue blindly believing that his boyfriend was a decent person.

Callum came over and tapped on my open door with a concerned expression. "Is everything okay? Elias was crying when he left."

"He'll be fine. He was just embarrassed he made a mistake." I pulled out my phone and sent a quick text to Jules demanding he meet me for lunch at my apartment. After the dual visits from Josh and Elias, I needed an attitude adjustment. "I have to take care of something outside of the office, but I'm not sure how long it'll take. I might not be back today. If anything comes up, shoot me an email, okay?"

"Sure thing."

I pocketed my phone and checked to make sure I had my keys before I left work to restore my former good mood.

IT FELT like it took forever before I heard Jules call out, "Xander, are you here?"

"Back in the bedroom!"

My anticipation built as he drew closer. "What was so important that I had to leave my office early to —*holy fucking hell*!"

Naked and facedown on my knees with my ass up in the air, I withdrew my lubed fingers from working my hole to prepare for Jules's arrival. I smirked into my white sheets as I wiped my hand clean on a towel, knowing I was presenting quite a sight. "You're late."

The sound of his clothes hitting the floor as fast as he could shed them amused me. "I'm not even going to ask."

"Great. Fuck now, talk later works for me."

My pulse spiked when I heard him open the condom packet I had left on the sheets. "How do you want it?"

"Hard enough that I'll be squirming in my seat when I return to work."

"Do you ever want it any other way?"

I didn't bother answering. As soon as he penetrated me, I shoved back hard, taking him deep. I rutted against him as he once again gave me the rough aggression I desperately needed after being visited by Josh and Elias. Jules chased all thoughts of them out of my mind as he fucked me, alternating between short and long thrusts that had me arching in pleasure.

When I tried to stroke my neglected erection, he pulled my hand away by my wrist and pinned it against the bed. It only turned me on more as I rubbed my cock against the sheets in desperate need of relief. I groaned with frustration as my lust spiraled at a dizzyingly fast speed, leaving me gasping for more. "Please, Julie, I'm begging you, touch me, *please!*"

"I appreciate you think I'm that good at multitasking, but—"

"Stop, stop, stop." I was grateful that he obeyed and pulled out of me without a complaint. Most of my exes wouldn't have given me that same courtesy.

With effort, I turned over and shoved him into a kneeling position, then clambered on top of him. I reached back to steady his cock as I slid onto it as he helped guide it into me. After that, I resumed our fierce pace as I gripped his shoulders and started bouncing down hard as he thrust up into me. Damn, I forgot how incredible it was to have all the stress fucked out of me. It was even better because we were doing it in the bed I had shared with Josh for six years. That would show the bastard.

I cried out Jules's name when he reached between us and began roughly jerking me off at the same time. It only took a few tugs before I came on his stomach and chest with a shout. I kept moving my hips as I leaned forward and kissed him hard, moaning into his mouth as his tongue drove me wild. Nothing else mattered as he gave me what I needed without question.

That was why it was such a surprise to suddenly find myself empty and flat on my back with him braced over me. "Now, it's my turn."

Rather than the aggressive fuck I had been enjoying, Jules slowed things down as he took his time kissing down my neck and chest. He teased my body with featherlight touches everywhere, reviving my lust with his gentle worship of every inch of me. I was shaking when he reached my cock, which he licked clean from my earlier release. He was meticulous as he made his way up my stomach, stopping to toy with each of my nipples until they pebbled under his attention. I trembled with need as he circled his fingers around my hole but denied me whenever I tried to force them inside me. It was exquisite torture. "*Julie.*"

He slid back into me nice and slow, savoring our bodies joining together. Instead of going hard and fast, he worked my body with a tenderness unlike anything I had ever experienced before. I wrapped my arms and legs around him as I drowned in his kisses. My body moved in sync with his as he rocked his hips against me, pushing me higher into a new level of ecstasy I hadn't known existed.

I gasped when he stroked my renewed arousal. As he pushed into me with a little more force, I braced my feet on the bed as I arched up into it, desperate for more of him. My toes curled in the sheets as I made needy noises, right on the edge again. He took me over when he slid all the way in as he reverently moaned, "*Xan*."

When he came, I climaxed a second time, overwhelmed by how much he cared about me and not just his own pleasure. He gave me a whisper-soft kiss that melted me further as I lost myself in his gentleness. It made me feel things for Jules I couldn't afford to in a friends-with-benefits relationship. For that reason, I forced myself to ignore the whispers that warned I was already in too deep.

ONE NAP AND A SANDWICH LATER, Jules and I canoodled on my living room couch after I decided against returning to work for the day. It was a pleasure Josh had denied me, and I hadn't realized how touch starved I was until Jules held me close. He stroked my hair like I was a cat, making me understand why they purred. I basked in the quiet affection. Jules's gentle caresses restored me, healing my old hurts in a way I hadn't thought would be possible a mere week after my six-year relationship died an inglorious death. I wanted to stay wrapped up in his comfort forever, because our friendship was more loving than any romantic partnership I had ever had with a previous boyfriend. Not for the first time did I wonder why the hell wasn't I dating Jules instead of wasting time with assholes who never treated me as well as him.

His soft voice pulled me from my thoughts. "Are you ready to talk about what happened earlier?"

"Hmm?" I shivered when Jules's fingers moved from my hair to trace the shell of my ear. It sent lust racing through me, even as it soothed me.

"While I appreciate your afternoon delight surprise," he said with a laugh, "you normally aren't someone who shirks work for sex. What happened?"

That was the one downside of being so close; Jules could always see straight through my bullshit. Instead of answering, I closed my eyes with a sigh as I focused on the way he trailed his fingers along my neck and raised chills on my skin. For such a simple touch, it felt incredible.

His hand stilled as he asked, "Is this making it too hard to think?"

"Please don't stop." I never wanted him to stop touching me.

He carded his fingers through my hair. "Then start talking."

I hated ruining the peaceful mood by bringing up what had happened earlier at my office. It was strange how it seemed like a lifetime ago after being with Jules, even though only a few hours had passed. But I wanted him to keep touching me more than I didn't want to explain the events leading up to our fun afternoon. "Josh stopped in for a visit to harass me about going to the wedding with Elias."

Jules stiffened under me, but he continued caressing my hair as I rested my head on his shoulder. "I sincerely hope you told him to go fuck himself with a cactus."

"No, but I did the next best thing. I said I was much happier with my new boyfriend who knew how to pleasure me better than *he* ever did."

I loved Jules's rumbling chuckle. "You seriously said that to his face?"

"Not in those exact words, but he got the gist loud and clear judging by his expression. Oh, and I also told him I should thank him for the breakup, since leaving him was the best thing that's happened to me. He stormed off fuming mad, as per usual. It was fantastic—right until he sent Elias in to see me afterward under some bullshit pretenses."

Jules tensed with an irritated growl, protectively hugging me closer. "It's bad enough that he cheated on you, but to rub it in your face like that—"

I interrupted his rant. "No, I'm glad he did it."

"Wait, what? Why?"

"Don't get me wrong. I'm still super fucking pissed at Josh for what he was trying to do by forcing Elias to visit me. But the poor guy is just a pawn in Josh's game, who's in way over his head. I don't know whether he'll listen to me, but it at least gave me the opportunity to warn him about what kind of bastard he's dating."

Jules sounded incredulous. "Warn him? Why bother? He deserves whatever Josh—"

"No, he doesn't. Nobody deserves that." I sat up to look Jules in the eyes. "As easy as it would be to blame Elias, it's not his fault that Josh is a cheating piece of shit. Josh fed him the same lies he told me when we got together, and Elias believed them like I did six years ago. Trust me, after knowing Elias for almost two years, he is too timid and shy to have actively set out to seduce Josh away from me. Josh cheated because he wanted to, and Elias was an easy target. He had no idea what he was getting into."

"Are you sure you aren't giving him too much credit for being innocent?"

I couldn't blame Jules for being suspicious when he didn't know Elias personally. "Elias reminds me of Callum. They have that same pure heart, but he wasn't lucky enough to find his Rune. He got stuck with my asshole ex, who'll date him for as long as it takes to win over daddy dearest. Once Josh secures his promotion, he'll cheat on Elias, too, if he isn't already."

The sadness in Jules's blue eyes moved my heart as he caressed my cheek. "You're right. Nobody deserves that."

"I hate getting my personal life involved with work. But the thought of Josh getting away with this and stealing six years of happiness from someone as nice as Elias makes me sick. I'm not sure if what I told him will make a difference or not, but I had to say something to warn him. Elias should be with someone who loves him for the sweet guy that he is and not use him because of who his dad is."

Jules reached out and pulled me into his lap for a tight hug. I returned the embrace, hiding my face against his neck and soaking up the comfort. The more I thought about Josh using Elias, the more it bothered me. When had I gotten so soft as to care about the person my ex-boyfriend had cheated on me with?

He made my heart flutter when he kissed my temple. "For Elias's sake, I hope he listens to you."

"I don't know, maybe he'll assume I'm a bitter ex trying to get revenge by making up lies about Josh and ignore me," I muttered. "Maybe I did the wrong thing. What if my warning him makes him double down in his commitment to Josh?"

Guiding me to look at him, Jules brushed my cheeks with his thumbs as he cradled my face in his hands. "Realistically, if they're living together now, he won't leave him tonight. But if he has at least half a brain, he'll see how Josh treats you at the wedding this weekend and realize you were right about everything. Hopefully, that'll be enough to get him to kick Josh's lying ass into the dumpster where he belongs."

"Oh, Elias mentioned Josh said I left him months ago for you. Josh will absolutely lose his shit when he sees you with me. Although, I guess us being 'together' will make Elias think Josh was right? Hmm."

"Josh will be so busy self-destructing in his impotent rage that it won't make much of a difference. If nothing else, his overt attempts to use Elias to make you jealous will surely ring some alarm bells for him."

A thought occurred to me that made me laugh. "Can you imagine if Josh is so angry about seeing me with you it makes him want me back just to spite you?"

"I take great pleasure in knowing he hates me that much, because the feeling is quite fucking mutual. As far as I'm concerned, he can go fellate a pufferfish. I'm not giving you up so he can have you back."

The comment caused me to arch an eyebrow. "I'm not your actual boyfriend, you know."

He scowled at my correction. "I'm just saying, as your longtime best friend and temporary fake boyfriend, I love you too much to stand by and watch you be miserable with him again. If Elias deserves better than Josh, so do you."

Even though I knew he meant love in a platonic sense, his words still suffused me with a warm glow of affection for him. "Don't worry, Julie. I'm happier in our fake relationship than I ever was in my real one with Josh. There's nothing he could say or do that would make me take him back. I'll take our friends-with-benefits arrangement over a romantic relationship with him any day of the week."

"Good." Jules kissed me, tantalizing me with a hint of possessiveness in his actions.

As we continued making out on my couch, I wasn't sure if anyone would be worth giving up what I had with Jules. That thought probably should have worried me, but as his hands wandered and heightened my pleasure, I forgot all about it.

Chapter Six

JULES

ON RHYS and Lucien's wedding day, I stood outside the cathedral with my brother while we waited to enter. Given who he was, it wasn't a surprise that people kept pointing over at us, craning their necks to get a peek at him.

Rune ignored the curious glances as he looked around at the enormous crowd waiting to be let inside the church. "Wow, there have to be at least five hundred people here."

Callum came over to join us. "It looks like it, but there's only three hundred. Thankfully, Rhys and Lucien invited enough famous clients that no one should harass you. Xander and I personally made sure everyone agreed to the policy of no autographs or photos of anyone attending the wedding and reception."

"If people actually obey that, I'll be impressed."

Rune wrapped his arm around Callum to hold him close. They were so sweet together. "Is everything okay?"

"Yeah, checked with Xander and Rhys to make sure they didn't need anything before the wedding got started. Brody and Augie are helping with last-minute groomsmen plans, so we probably won't see them until the reception. Xander promised he'd join us soon, though."

I snorted at that. "I'll believe that when it happens. He's too much of a perfectionist to leave anything half-done."

"He told me that was exactly what you would say, and he wanted me to remind you that he was committed to making a grand entrance. Whatever that means."

Before I could respond, I noticed Josh holding hands with an overwhelmed shorter man. Even at a distance, I could see how handsome he was. The sunlight made his hair seem almost white, and he looked damn fine in his black suit and green tie. I hated to admit it, but they were a gorgeous couple, minus the part where Josh was clearly ignoring Elias as he searched the crowd for Xander. His eyes narrowed when he caught sight of me, his rage momentarily going apoplectic before he got back in control of himself. He headed toward me, dragging poor Elias behind him with a death grip on his hand.

"Brace yourselves. The asshole has decided to

grace us with his presence," I muttered to Rune and Callum.

"That's Josh?" My brother scoffed. "I thought Xander had better taste than that."

Callum looked puzzled. "What do you mean?"

Because of their working relationship, Xander had requested Rune and I not to give him any details about his dating life. I offered a silent apology to my best friend, because Callum was about to get the full story.

"I'll explain later, baby," Rune murmured to his boyfriend.

As soon as Josh was close enough, I smiled at him with all the smarmy charm I knew he hated. "Why, look who it is."

"*Julian.*" He spat my name like it was the foulest word he had ever spoken, seething with anger. "Why are *you* here?"

"Because I was invited, *Joshua.*" I loved how pissed off he was at the fact I had the audacity to exist in the same space as him. Although Elias was almost hiding behind Josh, I held out my hand to him to shake. Josh jerked him away before we made contact. "That's a bit of an overreaction, don't you think? I was only trying to introduce myself."

"Don't touch him! Don't even look at him!"

Rune snickered at the reaction. "Good thing you never tried that caveman shit with Xander. He would have handed you your ass for that." God, I loved my smart-mouthed little brother so much.

"And who the fuck are you to tell me that—" Josh's words died in his mouth when he saw who he was talking to.

Rune's smirk was patronizing. "I'm going to guess based on your reaction, you know exactly who the fuck I am. Care to introduce us to your shadow?"

Josh stubbornly set his jaw and said nothing.

Callum's eyebrows furrowed with concern over the exchange, and I couldn't blame him. The whole thing was troubling. "Elias?"

After taking a deep breath, Elias stepped from behind Josh. The poor guy was shaking like a leaf. Xander's description of him being too timid to seduce Josh made a hell of a lot more sense to me. I didn't even know the guy, and I wanted to get him away from the asshole now. "Hi, Callum. It's good to see you again." He adjusted his glasses up the bridge of his nose. "Um, hello. I'm Elias. This is Josh. He's one of the attorneys at our office."

I found it interesting that Elias introduced him that way. Perhaps Xander had gotten through to him after all.

Josh slung his arm over Elias's shoulder and pulled him backward. I didn't like how his actions made Elias flinch. "I'm also his boyfriend."

Callum's gaze darted between Josh giving me a

death glare and Elias's defeated expression. "Elias, is everything okay?"

Josh answered for him. "It's great."

"I asked *him*." Rune had told me about Callum's protective streak, but it was the first time I had ever seen it in person. The Callum I had first met never would have been able to talk back to Josh. "Actually, while I have you here, Elias, could I ask you some questions about the Davros acquisition? Rhys has some last-minute requests he brought up with me earlier this morning, and I want to talk to you about it before I forget."

"Sure."

"Let's go over there and talk about it privately," Callum suggested, gesturing to some vague area to the right.

When Elias tried to walk away, Josh yanked him back. "You don't need to work when you're at a wedding. It can wait until Monday."

I didn't like the picture I was getting of how Xander would have been treated if he didn't have the backbone to stand up to Josh. No wonder Xander was so worried about the poor kid.

To my surprise, Elias pushed Josh's arm off his shoulder. "No, it's fine. I don't mind." He darted away to Callum before he could get captured again, and the two of them walked off together. It was a relief that Elias had temporarily escaped. Maybe Callum could talk some sense into him while he was at it. Thanks to his relationship with my brother, he had gained a lot more self-confidence.

With Elias out of the picture, Josh turned his full hatred onto me once more. He glared at me like he was trying to set me on fire with his mind. "Where's Xander?"

It didn't surprise me at all that was his first concern, but it still pissed me off. "He's no longer any of your business."

Josh demanded through gritted teeth, "Where. Is. He?"

"You ask that question like you have a right to know."

"Tell me!"

There wasn't a snowball's chance in hell I would do that. "In case you forgot, you chose that mouse over Xander." I gestured over to where Callum and Elias were talking to each other. "You forfeited your privilege to care about him when you cheated, so stop with the theatrics. He's moved on. You should do the same."

Josh balled his hands into fists like he wanted to hit me. "Who's his new boyfriend?"

"Wow, you really don't get it, do you?"

"There you are!" With impeccable timing, Xander walked over to us. The sight of him in his black suit, silver brocade vest, black shirt, and lavender tie was breathtaking. Every inch of him was perfect, down to his matching pocket square. I was so busy appreciating how gorgeous he was that I momentarily forgot about Josh. Xander slipped his arm around my waist and pulled me closer to kiss my cheek. I wrapped my arm over his shoulder and gave him a hug. "Sorry I'm late, babe."

"Not a problem, muffin." I kissed the top of his head because I knew it would piss off Josh, who wasn't tall enough to do that to Xander. His Napoleon complex had always amused me. "Everything okay?"

"Yeah, we should—"

Josh screeched loud enough to turn several heads around us, "*He's* your new boyfriend? *Him*?" Elias looked terrified, but he stayed with Callum.

"After almost twenty years of people assuming Julie was my boyfriend, I figured there must be a reason. Now that we're together, I understand the love that everyone saw between us." He gave me a sweet, lingering kiss on the lips that set off an explosion of rage in Josh. When he took a step toward us, Rune stepped in his way to make him back off. "I don't know what you're so upset about. You always thought Julie and I should be together."

"No, I thought you *were* together," he spat. "That's different."

"Well, unlike you, I waited until I was single to explore a new relationship." It was so satisfying watching Xander get back at Josh. I knew it made both of us petty bastards, but it felt great. "They've opened the doors to let people in. You should go."

Josh tried to argue, but Xander stared him down with a dismissive look that was so cold, it could have frozen over Hell. He had no choice but to withdraw and storm off, barking at Elias to join him. When Elias trudged over to meet him, Callum rejoined us.

Xander moved to the front to hug me properly. I held him close, ecstatic that he had chosen me over Josh, even if it was a fake relationship. He moaned for my ears only, "I could fuck you right here for doing this."

Me and my dick were immediately interested. "I'm sure there's a supply closet somewhere we can borrow."

"Don't tempt me when the wedding is about to start." He drew back, and I tried to calm myself. The last thing I wanted to do was walk into a church with a hard-on. I wasn't religious, but I was pretty sure that was a cardinal sin.

"What did you tell Elias?" Rune asked his boyfriend.

"I told him that wasn't love and he deserved better than that awful brute." Callum still looked troubled by the encounter. "He said he was starting to realize that."

"I'm glad you talked to him, baby." Rune took Callum's hand in his and brought it up to place a kiss on the back of it. "If he's smart, he'll listen to you."

"He didn't introduce that asshole as his boyfriend, so maybe there's hope for him yet," I added.

Callum's concern morphed into excitement. "Does this mean the two of you are officially dating now?"

"As opposed to unofficially?" His hopeful expression made me wish we had a better answer for him. "Sorry to disappoint you, but it's all for show."

"Oh." Callum couldn't hide his crestfallen expression.

Rune shifted his attention to me and Xander. "You know you're both a little too good at pretending to date each other, right? Because that looked way more real than fake."

Xander shrugged. "You say that like it's a bad thing."

"It's merely an observation."

"We should start heading into the chapel. The wedding will begin soon."

Rune gave Xander a look that said he wasn't buying the avoidance technique, but he kept his opinions to himself as he walked to the cathedral with Callum.

Xander stopped me from following them. "By the way, *muffin*? Really?"

"I'm hungry and it was the first word that popped into my head. Plus, *babe*? Seriously?"

He held my hand and bumped against my arm as we started heading toward the church. "I couldn't exactly walk over and say, 'Hey, sexy,' because you would have cracked up and given away that we were faking it."

I snickered as we walked up the cathedral steps. "Yeah, I definitely wouldn't have been able to keep a straight face if you did that. I guess we can stick with 'babe' for now."

"You should revise your choice of nicknames. I'm a lot of things, but I'm not a 'muffin.'"

"Okay, cookie."

"Julian!"

It was too much fun to tease him. "Quiche?"

He rolled his eyes as we entered the building. "Why does it have to be food related?"

"I told you, I'm hungry. So, that rules out 'kumquat,' then. What would you prefer, sweetums? Something cutesy?"

As we waited in line to enter the chapel, he tried to give me an annoyed look. The smile tugging at the corner of his lips ruined the effect.

I continued teasing him. "Baby cakes?"

"That's still food."

"I guess that means 'honey bun' is off the table, too? You're not leaving me with a lot of options, schmoopy."

He burst into laughter before quieting his amusement. "Okay, maybe I was better off with food."

"I'm glad you see it my way, pumpkin."

Xander tutted in indignation as we moved

forward in line. "What about me says giant orange gourd to you?"

"Yeah, you're right. You're kind of cute like a dumpling, though."

"Excuse you, I am *much* cuter than a dumpling. 'Kind of cute'? Please." His offended scoff was adorable. "You better try that again."

It was so much fun ruffling his feathers sometimes. "Fine, does 'cutie patootie' meet your exactingly high standards?"

"No, not at all."

"All right, back to food, cupcake." He made an aggrieved noise. "What if we change 'muffin' into 'stud muffin' instead?"

"Oh, *please* explain to me how a virile male horse combined with a pastry reminds you of me. I can't wait to hear this."

I grinned. "That's probably an explanation that I shouldn't make in a church."

Xander leaned closer to murmur, "That's real rich coming from the man who was down to fuck me in a church broom closet a few minutes ago."

"I still am. You want to go find out if there's one down that hall?"

He shoved my arm as we entered the chapel portion of the cathedral. It was an impressive feat of architecture, with the high coffered ceiling and expansive stained-glass windows making for a beautiful venue for a wedding. It was enough to distract me from our game for a moment. "Wow. This place is stunning."

"It is."

As we walked down the aisle hand in hand, it gave me a funny flutter in my heart thinking about doing that with Xander for real someday. It was a thought I shouldn't have about a fake boyfriend, but it curled up in my heart and wouldn't leave.

Xander pulled me from my thoughts as we continued walking to the front. "It must be a holy miracle. You ran out of pet names. Hallelujah."

"Don't start celebrating yet, kitten."

He groaned as we took a seat in the pews next to Callum and Rune. "Please, don't start with animal names."

"Why, is 'kitty' not cute enough for you, sweetie? Would you rather 'pigeon' instead?"

"You're not going to let this go, are you?"

I took much joy in reminding him of his part in inspiring the conversation. "Hey, you started this, jelly bean."

He hid his face against my shoulder as he tried to control his laughter. "Stop, you're killing me with all these names."

"Well, I can't call you 'hubby,' because we're not married yet."

"Even when we get—*if* we get married, you're not calling me that." His cheeks flushed at his slip of the tongue.

Now, *that* was interesting. It looked like I wasn't the only one who had matrimonial ideas from walking down the aisle together.

He tried to recover from his flub. "You're about two bad nicknames away from calling me 'meatball,' so you have two final chances to pick something before you're banned from pet names forever."

I rubbed my chin and pretended to think about it. "You know, 'meatball' isn't half-bad. I—"

"*No.*"

Drawing inspiration from our surroundings, I tried another name. "Angel?"

He snorted at that one. "We both know I am anything but."

"So it'll be ironic, then. How very hipster of you, angel."

"Nope, I reject it. Here's your last shot not to screw it up."

I braced my arm on the back of the pew and rested my hand on his shoulder as I held him. "Fine, from now on, you'll be my pookie."

"*Pookie?*" I loved how scandalized he sounded. "You are *not* calling me '*pookie.*'"

"Give me one good reason why I can't."

"Because it sounds like 'poke me,' for starters."

Leaning closer, I said in a suggestive voice next to his ear, "See? It's perfect. I can't wait to poke you later, pookie." For good measure, I tugged on his earlobe with my teeth.

My joke earned me an elbow jab to the ribs that was hard enough to make me wheeze. That was fair. I definitely deserved it.

"You're *so* going to Hell for saying that in a church."

"It's totally worth it, pookie."

He heaved a long-suffering sigh, but his amused grin betrayed him. I rubbed his shoulder with my thumb in apology, smiling when he reached up to stroke my hand in silent acknowledgement.

While I wasn't a religious man by any means, I nevertheless offered a prayer of gratitude for having someone as incredible as Xander as my best friend. I tried not to notice when I accidentally made a second one, wishing that things between us would become real instead of staying pretend.

Chapter Seven

XANDER

AS RHYS and Lucien exchanged their vows during the ceremony, it occurred to me that going to a wedding two weeks after ending a six-year relationship should be hell. But their fairy-tale romance was too beautiful to inspire bitterness. I was glad that they had found true love within their lifelong friendship, but it was hard not to compare my situation with my own best friend.

When I was eight years old, I moved next door to Jules and Rune with my mom after my parents divorced. Between their sky-high expectations of me and watching their marriage fall apart, I had been a pint-sized perfectionist and control freak from a very early age. Jules had been the polar opposite of me; he was a whirlwind of chaos trapped in the body of a small boy. He had been messy, without a single care in the world, and completely unconcerned with consequences. Our differences both repulsed and intrigued me when we first met. His warmth quickly won me over, despite my initial reservations. It had blown my mind that he could laugh it off whenever he messed up something. I was the type to beat myself up for days if I got an A instead of an A+ on a test. Jules refused to conform to any of the rules I lived by, and he was the only person who never demanded perfection from me. He also never made fun of me for needing to be the way I was.

Both of my parents were uptight, emotionally repressed, and physically distant. That's why Jules's insistence on hugging me every time we met and parted had confused me. I couldn't understand his need for what I thought was a pointless gesture. But I gained a new perspective after my mom's car accident on her way to work when I was nine.

For the entire day, I emotionlessly soldiered on like I had been raised to do. My father refused to take me, so I stayed at Jules's house while they kept my mother overnight for observation. Once we were alone in his room, he hugged me. Instead of the quick hello and goodbye hugs I was used to, he held me tight and told me it was okay to be sad. No one had ever given me permission before to be upset; I was always instructed to suck it up by my parents. It was the first time I cried in front of him, but he never let me go as I sobbed years of repressed tears. And when I eventually regained control of my emotions, he made me laugh so hard I forgot to feel embarrassed about it. We fell asleep in bed together that night, and after that, we were inseparable. I also became a hug addict with Jules, craving that close bond that only we shared.

Jules was the one person who never judged me for having emotions I didn't want to show to the world. He thought I was perfect, even when I fucked up. No matter how awful things got, he was there with a hug and a smile to make me laugh and feel better. I could count on him for anything and he would never let me down. My trust in him was absolute. He was my most important person, and I'd be lost without him as the safe harbor that kept me steady when life overwhelmed me. There was nothing I wouldn't do for him.

We had been laughing off people thinking we were dating since we were in high school. But after almost twenty years of treating it as a joke, watching Rhys and Lucien celebrating their love forced me to question if maybe we should take it seriously. The past eight days of our friends-with-benefits relationship had been beyond incredible. However, walking down the aisle as he teased me about pet names caused me to wonder whether there was more to us than we were willing to admit.

At the reception, I rested my head on Jules's shoulder as we watched Rhys and Lucien have their first dance to Jason Mraz and Colbie Caillat's

"Lucky." It was wonderful watching them hold each other with so much love while making each other laugh. What was strange was I could easily picture dancing with Jules at our reception, while I never considered marrying Josh after being together for six years.

My gaze drifted over to the table on the far side of the enormous banquet hall to where I stuck him with Elias. When he noticed my attention, he tried to kiss his boyfriend, who jerked back to prevent it. Josh's aggression intensified to a scary level, and I grew uncomfortable when he went for Elias's neck instead.

I was no stranger to Josh's anger issues. The last year of our relationship had been bad, because he sensed me pulling away from him and attempted to exert control to keep me. I never had a problem standing up to him or his temper. It was easy for me to argue my way to victory with logic and make him stomp off to sulk for a few days. The number of times Josh had stormed out of a room after losing an argument with me had entertained me. Outside the cathedral before the wedding was yet another instance of him ending a disagreement like a spoiled toddler taking his toys and going home. But Elias seemed to be too timid to fight back, which troubled me.

Returning my attention to my boss and his husband, I smiled when I saw Rhys looking up at Lucien with complete adoration. They kissed when the song ended, earning loud cheers and applause.

Even Rhys's parents were clapping, despite their initial horrified reactions to finding out he eloped with Lucien last year. I was glad they had reconciled, since I knew it meant a lot to Rhys. He and his father still had a long way to go to patching up their relationship, but attending the wedding was a huge step.

"That was so beautiful," Callum said, wiping away tears from the corners of his eyes as Rhys and Lucien walked off the dance floor holding hands. It was adorable seeing him so moved by our boss's marriage. He always appreciated the little moments in life that were so easy to overlook. "It was totally worth all the last-minute headaches trying to put this together."

"Agreed." While it had been irritating dealing with wedding planning on top of my normal responsibilities, everything had been perfect for Rhys and Lucien so far.

The white rose and blue-purple dendrobium orchid centerpieces on every table that matched their boutonnières was my favorite touch. They had been on the ends of each pew in the church, too. The banquet room was decorated in the same color tones, and it was one of the most beautiful wedding receptions I had ever attended. It should be, since it cost a fortune.

Jules kissed my temple, making something flutter inside me. "You both did a fantastic job. Everything is gorgeous."

"Rhys is damn lucky to have the two of you taking such excellent care of him," Rune added. "Especially since you got Renée to cater the event." She was a Michelin-star chef that ran the award-winning Ambrosia restaurant with her wife, Maria. They were both good friends with the four of us and had quickly adopted Rhys and Lucien into their inner circle once we introduced them.

"Don't forget about the cake! It's one of the best I've tasted." Callum bounced with excitement at the prospect. He shared a love for all things sweet with our boss, so Rhys had let Callum join him and Lucien as the arbitrator when they did their taste testing. You would have thought he received a million-dollar bonus with how ecstatic he was for that opportunity. "Rhys promised I could have two slices to thank me for helping them pick it out."

Rune chuckled as he looked at Callum with all the love he held in his heart for his boyfriend. He had always been a quiet loner who believed true love didn't exist. However, Callum had brought sunshine into his gloomy world and changed him for the better. They both had grown so much over their months of being together, and it was great seeing them deeply in love with each other. I was proud of Rune for letting love into his life after so many years alone. He was like a little brother to me since I'd met him when he was five.

When Jules looked over at me, I saw that same

love in his eyes. It had nothing to do with being my fake boyfriend to piss off my ex. He regarded me with genuine affection and adoration, which I reciprocated. The question wasn't how we felt about each other; it was what the hell were we going to do about it?

DINNER HAD BEEN OUTSTANDING, proving Renée was a culinary master who deserved all her accolades and then some. As people finished, they began hitting the dance floor and mingling to chat with friends. Rhys and Lucien worked their way through the tables until they reached ours.

They both looked incredible. Rhys wore a white tuxedo while Lucien was in a black one. They both had a single white rose with two blue-purple dendrobium orchids as boutonnières in their lapels. Their cheeks were flushed as they held hands, love radiating off them in waves. It was a glorious thing to behold.

"Congratulations to the both of you," I said. "It's been wonderful celebrating with you today."

Rhys was all smiles. "We owe you and Callum so much for helping with all the planning. I know it was a big ask on top of everything else, but you both outdid yourselves."

Callum blushed at the compliment. "We were

happy to help, although the wedding planner did most of it. It wasn't all us."

"True, but you two were the ones who made sure all the little details were perfect."

Lucien moved his glasses up the bridge of his nose. "We both appreciate your efforts. You went above and beyond, which means a lot. Plus, you kept Rhys from stressing about the small stuff, which I can't thank you enough for. Not to mention introducing us to Renée, who did an incredible job with the food tonight."

"I will say, eloping was way less stressful than throwing this grand wedding." Rhys laughed as he bumped shoulders with his husband. "But it would have been unbearable without your help, so thank you. You more than deserve your three-week vacation after this."

To show gratitude for our efforts, Rhys had given Callum and me three weeks off while he would be out of the office on his honeymoon in the Maldives. The workaholic in me would stop in a few times after hours just to make sure there were no pressing emergencies, but the gesture was still nice. It was another example of Rhys's generosity. After I had to call off all the plans for his wedding with Olivia last year, he had gifted me a five-thousand-dollar bonus. He also gave Jules a grand for going over to his house to help get the locks changed while he was away in Greece.

Rhys shifted his attention over to me. "By the way,

I know you're the consummate professional, but I have no problem with you being more open about your relationship. As many times as people have seen Lucien kiss me goodbye at the office, it won't shock anybody if you do the same."

I tried not to die of mortification when Jules teased me. "See, pookie? I told you we could leave the door open."

My cheeks were flame red in embarrassment as I gave him a disapproving look. "*Julian.*"

"Ooh, I'm in trouble now."

Rhys was a chill enough boss to laugh about it. "Enjoy the rest of the reception! We'll stop by before the night's over to say goodbye."

Once they walked away, I wanted to reprimand Jules, but his broad grin disarmed my annoyance. "I can't believe you did that."

"Can't you, though?" How could I be mad when his cheekiness was so charming?

Rune chuckled. "I definitely can. The 'pookie' was a nice touch."

I rolled my eyes. "Please don't encourage him. He's bad enough as it is."

"And you love me for it." He kissed me into silence, before I could fully process what he said. When his tongue sought entrance, I denied him as punishment. He laughed and looked entirely too pleased with himself. "That gives me an idea, actually. We'll be back."

Before I could ask what he meant, Jules grabbed my hand in his and led me toward the exit. I noticed Josh never took his eyes off us until we stepped into the hallway and out of sight. To my surprise, Jules didn't let go. He continued leading me down the long corridor and turned the corner. When we reached the supply closet, he tested the handle which was unlocked.

"The broom closet, Julian? Really?"

"Relax. We're not actually going to do anything." He flipped on the light as he ushered me into the small walk-in closet stuffed with supplies on shelves. Then, he left the door slightly ajar to illuminate a sliver of the dim hallway. Satisfied, he mussed his hair up as he returned his attention to me. I offered no resistance as he undid the button of my pants and unzipped them.

It was only when Jules pinned me to the wall that I asked, "What are you doing? Besides giving me naughty ideas."

"Putting on a show." His sexy smirk caused my heart to skip a beat, as did the sound of distant footsteps. "Look at that, the bastard is right on time."

I shivered as Jules started kissing up my neck, the pieces clicking into place about his plan to piss off Josh. My petty side reveled in what was about to happen, even if it was immature.

We heard Josh mutter in the distance, "I'll kill that fucking asshole for stealing Xander from me!"

Indignation flared at his words. Did that delusional idiot really think Jules was the reason we weren't together anymore? How could he possibly lack that much self-awareness to not understand that him cheating on me was why we broke up? Not to mention all the years of misery we endured.

"Now would be a fantastic time to moan," Jules suggested.

Oh, I would do more than that. I would get the ultimate payback on my asshole ex for what he had done to me. "Let's make him *really* mad. Blow me."

Jules pulled back to look at me with excitement. "You mean for real?"

The thought of Josh walking in on Jules going down on me made me rock-hard in an instant. I pressed against him so he could feel my arousal and begged loud enough to be heard in the hallway, "Please!" Josh swore, his voice sounding closer than before. I rubbed my erection against Jules's thigh that he had worked between my legs, desperate to get off with the ultimate form of payback. "Please, Julie!"

Without a word, he dropped to his knees and tugged down my pants and purple underwear enough for my cock to spring free. As my dick slid into the slick heat of his mouth, I sighed with relief. I laced my fingers through Jules's blond hair, caressing him as he sucked me off in earnest. My head rested against the shelf behind me as I surrendered to him with a moan. He really was the best friend ever. The experience was also making me rethink my stance on public exhibitionism, because I now found it sexy as hell instead of distasteful.

My eyes fluttered shut for a moment as I focused on the pleasure Jules graciously bestowed upon me. He hollowed his cheeks as he worked my length with his magical mouth. It was only when I felt a malevolent presence that I remembered what was happening.

When I opened my eyes, I locked gazes with Josh, who was watching us through the slight crack we had deliberately left. My desire skyrocketed at getting caught. I refused to avert my gaze from him as I moaned, "So good, Julie!"

Josh's rage twisted his handsome face into an ugly and fearsome thing. He ripped the door open as he snarled, "What the fuck are you two doing?"

Jules let my hardness slip from his lips with a deliciously wet *pop* before looking over his shoulder at Josh with disdain. "Is there some reason you're interrupting us?"

"Get away from him!"

The sudden stop soured my mood. "You're neither needed nor wanted here, Josh. Go back to babysitting your boy toy so I can finish getting off."

"Have fun regretting that *this*," Jules said as he stroked my prick, "is all mine now because you're a fucking idiot. And unlike you, I actually know how to pleasure him."

Before Josh could respond, Jules resumed his blow

job. I gripped his shoulder hard, almost losing it as he deep-throated me with wild abandon. He drove all thoughts of Josh out of my mind by sucking my cock for everything it was worth. The sight of my dick sliding between my best friend's swollen lips was too much to handle. My muscles tensed as I whimpered, "Julie, I'm so close! *Fuck!*"

When Jules cupped my balls with a slight squeeze, I muffled my cry with my hand as I climaxed. He swallowed my release, then put on a show of licking me clean. I only remembered Josh was there when he slammed the door and stormed off in disgust, just like he always did when he lost a battle. It did nothing to diminish the glow of my satisfying orgasm. If anything, his rage made it even better.

Jules wiped the corner of his mouth as he stared up at me with an intense desire. I reached down and jerked him up by his tie so I could devour him with a needy kiss. The taste of myself on his tongue made me moan. I may have come, but I was still horny as hell from enraging Josh. "Tell me you have something with you so we can live out your fantasy of fucking in a broom closet."

He stepped back so he could reach over and lock the door, before pulling out condom and lube packets from his pocket. I used the opportunity to pull up my underwear and pants, allowing me to reposition myself next to the shelf on the opposite wall. "You should have been a Boy Scout."

His smirk turned me on more. "Nah, I don't need a merit badge to prove I'm skilled at tying knots."

"I was referring to always being prepared, but good to know for later." Facing away from Jules, I dropped my pants and spread my legs. It was the perfect position to show off my surprise for him.

He drew a sharp breath as he saw my bare ass being hugged by neon pink bands of my purple jockstrap underwear. After he mentioned dreaming about me in them, I couldn't resist making it a reality.

Jules caressed along the straps with an appreciative moan. "Mm, it's even better in real life. God, your ass is perfect."

I wiggled it to further tempt him. "Why don't you show me how much you appreciate it?"

He pulled my underwear down so he could have easier access. "I'll fuck you while you wear this later, don't worry."

"Can't wait."

My patience with being stretched and my need for instant gratification warred with each other. I put up with it for as long as I could bear. "Hurry up and fuck me before someone catches us."

Not needing to be told twice, Jules rolled on the condom and then positioned me so he could enter. I braced against the metal shelving in front of me as I pushed back against him, biting my lips to hold in a satisfied moan from him filling me. He started off with short and fast strokes, making me clutch the shelf as I held on tight while he fucked me just the way I liked it. The rough sound of our bodies connecting and the slick sounds of the lube sent my lust spiraling as I grew hard once more.

He gripped my hips, using the hold to guide his well-placed thrusts. My back arched from the satisfaction racing up my spine and down to my toes. He dominated my desires as I gave up total control and let him pound me into oblivion.

I bit my wrist to muffle a cry when he nipped at my ear. The pleasure was blinding as he took me with a fierceness that made me ache to shout for all to hear. But I continued smothering my sounds of enjoyment, not wanting anyone to interrupt us until I had gotten off a second time. That proved to be a challenge when he reached around and started jerking me off with rough tugs. The primal urges that drove me, as well as the smug gratification of knowing Josh was still fuming mad over me being with Jules, meant I wouldn't last long.

While I was lost in pleasure, a tiny part of my brain noticed once again, Jules was giving me everything I wanted without question. He knew what I needed without me having to ask, and he loved me enough to do it. Getting railed against a shelf was a weird time to realize my best friend was probably as in love with me as I was with him. However, that was a thought to process when more of me could focus on it.

Jules pushed in to the hilt, resting his head against mine as he gasped, "Xan," next to my ear. He pumped his hips as he came in spurts, hitting that spot within me that caused me to spill my seed again. We were both breathless as we finally paused from our frenetic rush toward ecstasy. My body hummed with sexual satisfaction as I enjoyed the immense high our aggressive coupling brought me.

I laughed when he grabbed a paper towel off the shelf over my shoulder to clean his hand. "Well, that's convenient." I did the same to wipe myself off. "Damn, that was *incredible*."

Jules threw away his used condom, the two packets, and his paper towel before he redressed. "Something tells me this won't be our last forbidden fuck."

While I never imagined I'd be into that kind of thing, it had been an enlightening experience. "I can't believe you made me regret turning down your offer to do this in a church."

"See? Imagine how much sexier it would have been to be sacrilegious on top of it."

After fixing my appearance, I turned to face him. He offered me a mint, making me laugh at how prepared he was. "Seriously, when did you turn into such a Boy Scout?"

He popped one into his mouth with a grin. "Aren't you proud of how organized I am?"

I wrapped my arms around his neck and enjoyed a minty fresh kiss with him. "I am. It looks like all of those years of getting after you about always being ready for anything have finally paid off."

"Ha, and you thought I never listened to you." He kissed me again, longer and slower this time, making me melt like the mint I just finished. "I'm willing to do anything for my pookie."

I huffed at the nickname, because it annoyed me that the obnoxious name was getting cuter. "Well, your pookie wants to go see if they're serving cake yet. Come on."

Jules stole one more kiss with a laugh, before we returned to the banquet hall holding hands. The warm glow of satisfaction between us could only come from love. Now, I needed to figure out a way to talk to him about it without ruining everything. But first, I wanted to enjoy some damn cake after working up an appetite.

Chapter Eight

JULES

THANKS TO THE OPEN BAR, the party was in high gear as the evening wore on at the wedding reception. After our supply closet escapades, Xander had been in a fantastic mood. Not even the bullshit drama with Josh and Elias could bring him down. I was so proud.

He was currently cooing over pictures of Ambrose and Augie's kitten, Everest. They had rescued him while on vacation at a cabin last weekend for an early celebration of their one-year anniversary. Both of them were groomsmen in the wedding and looked dashing in their tuxedos. Rhys and Lucien eloping last year inspired them to evolve their friendship into a romantic one. It was yet another case where two longtime friends had gotten together and found happiness. I was surrounded by evidence that dating your best friend was a wonderful idea, but I wasn't sure if Xander would agree.

While I hadn't spent much time with Callum's brother and boyfriend, they were fun to hang out with whenever we had the chance. The way the two of them bantered with each other reminded me of Xander and myself. Rune and Augie had bonded over their shared love of cooking, which was great. It thrilled me my once loner brother had gained a social circle of genuine friends.

I enjoyed seeing Xander's soft side as he continued fussing over cat pictures. "He's so tiny!"

Ambrose flicked to the next image, setting off another round of *awww* reactions. "He won't stay wee for long."

The picture of a powder puff white kitten would have melted even the most frozen of hearts. It made me want a cat myself, as did the fact that Xander had always loved them. We had talked about getting one while we lived together after college, but we had never gone through with it. Maybe we could adopt one or two of them now, though. *Wait, aren't you getting a little ahead of yourself?*

"I'm so scared he'll get squished underfoot by Brody." Augie sighed when Ambrose laughed. "It's not funny! He's itty-bitty and you're a giant."

"If I haven't crushed you yet, Everest will be fine. He's a smart lad." It was a fair point, since Ambrose's tall, broad, and muscular build dwarfed Augie's slighter frame. Even I appeared on the smaller side next to him. "Besides, he's your shadow. If anyone will step on him, it'd be you."

"Trust me, I'm already paranoid enough about that as it is. I don't need you reminding me of that fact, thanks."

Ambrose leaned over and kissed Augie on the top of his head. "I keep telling you not to worry so much. You're a great cat dad." It was cute how it made him blush.

"I'm so sad you got Everest after I moved out." Callum pouted, before turning his pleading blue eyes on my poor brother, who didn't stand a chance of resisting. "Maybe we could get one sometime? If we adopted a girl kitten, we could call her Olympe after Olympe de Gouges. Wouldn't that be grand?"

Rune answered him with a passionate kiss that made Ambrose and Augie chuckle.

Based on my younger brother's reaction, I had my suspicion that the name was someone famous from the French Revolution. I had to hand it to Callum. He may have been guileless, but he also had Rune wrapped around his little finger.

My eyes drifted over to Josh's table and I frowned when both he and Elias were gone. After knowing that asshole for six years, there was no way he would have left the reception without coming over for one final gloat in front of Xander. There wasn't a chance in hell that he would let our little show from earlier go unpunished. It was always an eye for an eye with him.

The realization made my stomach drop out at what that possibly meant.

I glanced over at Xander, who seemed oblivious to the pair's disappearance and was brainstorming kitten names with Callum. Perhaps I was overreacting—and it definitely wasn't my business—but my gut was telling me I had to make sure. I leaned over and gave Xander a quick kiss as I said in his ear, "I'll be back."

He nodded and kept chatting with everyone as I got up and left the banquet hall. I returned to the hallway with the supply closet, where my worst suspicions were confirmed.

"Josh, no! I told you—stop it—I told you I don't want to do this! Let me go!"

My anger boiled over at the asshole's response. "You'd do this if you really loved me." Did he used to say that kind of thing to Xander, too? The thought made me sick.

"If you loved me, you wouldn't ask me to do this! I respect Xander and—no! Stop, you're hurting me!"

That was all I needed to hear to act. I threw the door open with a bang, enraged at the sight of Elias cowering in a corner. His shirt was unbuttoned and his pants undone as Josh trapped him in place with his larger body. Even his glasses were askew.

Josh's laughter was pure evil. "I knew you'd come for me, Xa—" When he whipped around and saw me instead, his triumphant expression morphed into something sinister. "What the fuck are *you* doing here?"

His malevolence was chilling, but my rage was hotter. "You have two seconds to get away from him, before I call security and have them throw your sorry ass out of this reception. And trust me, if you cause that kind of scene at Rhys's wedding, you can kiss that promotion you're chasing goodbye."

He shoved Elias aside, who hit a shelf hard with a yelp of pain. I couldn't spare him more than a glance, because the asshole charged at me in a show of aggression that was probably supposed to be intimidating. Too bad that wouldn't work on me.

I stared him down, knowing from Xander's stories over the years that the silent treatment unnerved Josh the most. It was sad how easy it was to rattle his unearned confidence as he tried to puff himself up to take me in a fight.

The moment dragged out into an uncomfortable silence. He was the first to break by snarling, "Say something, damn it!"

"You're lucky I'm nice enough to give you the option to leave quietly after what you've done to him. *Go.*"

"Why do you care about him? Is Xander not enough for you? You want to steal Elias from me, too?" He held his fists up in a poor imitation of a boxer in a movie. "I'll fucking take you right now. Come on!"

What the fuck kind of logic was that? How did he manage to be even dumber than I thought? An amoeba could put him to shame. "Before you make an even bigger ass out of yourself than you already have, I should warn you that I have a second-degree black belt in karate and six years of repressed anger I'd be *more* than happy to unleash on you for what you've done to Xander. Unless you want to end up in the hospital tonight, storm off like you always do, and go sulk it off. *Now.*" It was a good threat, but as much as I hated him, I'd never be able to follow through on it in good conscience.

He took a step closer, so I called his bluff. I pulled out my phone and used the audio command to trigger it without having to glance at it. "Call Xander."

I hit the speakerphone button as my phone's virtual assistant announced, *"Calling Xander."*

After the first ring, he spat, *"Fine.* Come on, Elias. We're leaving. I don't need to take bullshit from this asshole." I pretended to end the call, but I only shut off the screen to slip it into my jacket pocket, just in case shit went south.

"No." His voice was soft but had a quiet determination to it.

Josh whipped around to face him. "What the fuck do you mean *no?*"

Elias shook like a leaf in a windstorm as he stood his ground. "I mean no, I'm not coming with you. I'm not staying with you, either."

"You're breaking up with me?" It amazed me that Josh could sound so indignant about it after what he had done. "Are you fucking serious right now?"

While Elias's resolve didn't waver, he still shrunk back from Josh's anger. "I want you to get your things out of the apartment tonight and leave your key."

"You can't kick me out!"

"I can, and I am. You don't have much there. I want everything out by the time I get home tonight." It might have been a weird reaction, but I was oddly proud of Elias for standing up for himself.

"Fuck you! You can't throw me out on the streets!"

Elias took a deep breath to steady himself. "If—if you're still there, I'll call the police to report you for stalking and trespassing."

"An arrest would *definitely* fuck up your promotion plans," I cheerfully reminded him. "If I were you, I'd get your shit and go while you still have the option."

Josh's snarl was fearsome, making Elias tremble. But he spun on his heel and shoulder-checked me as he stomped out.

I couldn't resist one last dig. "Don't forget to slam the door on your way out."

As he had earlier, he slammed it so hard that it shook in the frame. I smirked until I saw Elias wince as if he had been physically struck. The enormity of what happened hit him and he hyperventilated, right on the verge of having a panic attack.

Even though I should hate him for being the

person Xander's ex cheated on him with, the poor bastard had been through the wringer today. I couldn't in good conscience leave him alone in such a state, so I approached him as I would a skittish animal.

The pain in his eyes broke my heart and made me understand why Xander couldn't be mad at Elias after what he had been through. I did what I always did when somebody needed comfort: I gathered him into a tight hug. "It's okay. You're safe now."

Elias burst into tears as he sobbed against my chest, clinging onto me as if I were a life raft in an ocean. If someone had told me I would hold the person who was partially responsible for Xander's breakup and offer them support, I never would have believed them. I held him as he cried, murmuring gentle words to help try to calm him down. Every time he whispered an apology, I shushed him.

He hid his face against my chest as he mumbled, "This is so embarrassing. I'm sorry for crying on you. You don't even know me."

I patted his back to reassure him. "You're fine. The only person who should be apologizing isn't here."

He bashfully looked up at me with his striking gray eyes. "Thank you for saving me."

"You saved yourself at the end. Good for you for kicking his pathetic ass to the curb with the rest of the trash where he belongs."

My comment made him crack a smile. It disappeared when the door opened, and we heard Xander's voice. "Jules, are you in—"

He stopped when he saw me hugging Elias, who flung himself out of my arms and into a shelf, knocking over some rolls of toilet paper. "X-Xander, this—this isn't what it looks like!" After he said that, I realized how bad it looked for me to be embracing him when he was half-undressed. "I wasn't trying to steal him, or—"

Xander shut the door behind him, making Elias flinch as he once again bordered on having an anxiety attack. "Elias." When he started hyperventilating again, Xander reached out to him and held on to his shoulders, giving them a comforting squeeze. "Calm down, and take a deep breath. I'm not mad at you."

He stared at Xander in shock. "Y-you're *not*? But it looks like we were—"

"About to have sex?" Xander couldn't keep the amusement out of his voice when Elias blushed. "Here's the thing. Out of everyone in this world, there is one person I trust above all others to never betray me. There isn't a man alive who could make Jules stray from me."

"He was comforting me after Josh—after he…"

"Jules gives the best hugs, which you look like you've needed all day. When I saw the two of you together, that was my only conclusion, okay? I know him too well and for too long to suspect him of cheating on me." His answer caused my pride to surge that he trusted in our bond that much. My heart also skipped a beat because he talked as if we were dating for real.

Elias sagged with relief as he clutched his shirt closed. "I was afraid after Josh cheated on you, and then you saw me with Jules that you'd assume I was trying to steal him, too."

"For starters, I don't think you stole Josh from me. If anything, I owe you a thank-you for helping me get out of that awful relationship."

I couldn't blame Elias for being mind-boggled by Xander's stance on the situation. He closed the buttons of his shirt and straightened his tie, unable to look my friend in the eyes. "Why are you being so nice to me about this? I don't deserve your understanding. You should hate me."

"We've known each other professionally for about two years, and in that time, we've had a cordial relationship, wouldn't you agree?"

"Yes, but——"

Xander talked over his protests. "You're polite, professional, and good at what you do. Out of all the attorneys on our legal team, you are by far the best. Although your father is lead counsel, you don't let that impact your job. You're a hard worker who never cuts corners."

Elias tucked his shirt back in his pants as he refastened them. "T-thanks, that's—that's very kind of you to say." He picked up the toilet paper he knocked over earlier to return it to its rightful place on the shelf. That small action said a lot about him.

"The Elias I have known for the last two years is not the type of man who would kick down Josh's door and seduce him with his wicked ways."

I couldn't help trying to lighten the mood further. "You mean with his masculine wiles?"

Xander gave me a teasing look. "Is there such a thing as masculine wiles?"

"It's sexist if you think wiles are just for women."

"Fair enough." He shifted his attention to Elias, who had regained his composure. "Whatever you call it, I know that's not who you are."

He still seemed troubled. "If I had known Josh had a boyfriend when he pursued me, I never would've agreed to be with him. It shocked me when he said you two dated in the past, because, well…"

"You assumed I was with Jules like everyone else?"

He nodded with sheepish embarrassment. "That's why when he told me you left him for Jules, I believed him."

"While we've known each other since we were kids, our relationship is a recent development."

It was too perfect of an opportunity to pass up. "Happy eighth-day anniversary, pookie." I blew him a kiss for good measure, loving the laugh it earned me.

"Anyway, the point is, you're a nice guy, Elias. My anger is aimed solely at Josh for what he did to me and that he dragged you into this mess. I meant it when I told you that you deserve better than him treating you so terribly. That's why I talked to you in my office, because I wish—" Xander cut himself off with a troubled expression that disappeared as fast as it arrived. "Because I wish someone had warned me about how terrible Josh was and could have saved me six years of aggravation. It's bad enough that he did it to me. I didn't want him to steal years of your happiness, too."

Elias teared up again. "Thank you, Xander. That you would still help me after everything, I can't tell you how much that means to me."

"I'm just relieved you broke up with him."

His eyebrows furrowed in confusion. "How did you know I did that?"

"Should we try to convince him we're telepathic?" I winked at Xander, having always loved teasing him about being able to read his thoughts.

"You ruined our chances of doing that since you said it out loud."

My grin was unrepentant. "Oops."

"To answer your question, Josh informed me when I had him escorted off the property."

Elias's jaw dropped. "You did *what?*"

"Jules left his phone on when he called me. I heard enough to get security to address the problem. On my way here with them, we encountered him in the hallway. They were all too happy to chuck him out for us, and there weren't any witnesses to report back to Rhys about what happened. He won't know about it, so today is still perfect for him and Lucien."

It was gratifying to know that Josh had faced consequences for his actions. I could have gone for round two with Xander if Elias wasn't with us.

"You did that for me?" He regarded Xander with awe. "Thank you."

"Why don't you go wash your face and come join us at our table when you're ready?"

"Is it really okay? I'd appreciate it, especially since all anyone wants to talk about at mine is golf. I *hate* golf."

Xander nodded. "I think Callum would also enjoy getting to chat with you more."

"I can't thank either of you enough for what you've done for me today."

"One more thing. If Josh gives you any problems at work, tell me. I'll have it dealt with."

He was being serious, but I chuckled. "When you say it that way, it sounds like you're going to have hit men put concrete shoes on him and boot his ass off a pier to sleep with the fish forever."

"It won't be quite *that* severe, but I'll have him taken care of."

"You still sound like you're having him offed." I mimicked a New Jersey mobster accent. "Next, you'll be telling me you know people."

Elias laughed, finally looking at ease. "I'll meet

you at your table later. Thanks again." He was considerate and closed the door as he left.

Before I could show Xander my appreciation for his beautiful follow-through, his troubled expression returned from before. I walked over to him. "What's wrong? You did a good thing tonight."

"I told him I wished someone had warned me about Josh. But then I remembered that you did. Repeatedly. You told me something was off about him, that he wasn't as nice as he seemed, that he was too controlling, and that we moved in together too fast. But I didn't listen because…"

"Because you're stubborn?" I asked in a teasing tone, not wanting him to beat himself up for things in the past.

He glanced away from me. "Because I thought you were jealous of him."

I guided him to meet my gaze. "You weren't wrong. I *was* jealous of him."

"But you were also right. If I had listened to you, I wouldn't have wasted the last six years of my life with him. I would have been happy with you."

"Yeah, until some other gorgeous guy came along." That thought stung more than it should have. He remained silent as he struggled with something. "What?"

"For six years, I stayed in a dead-end relationship I had no business being in. I don't want to waste any more of my life being unhappy with the wrong person." He took a steadying breath as he looked up at me with his beautiful green-hazel eyes. "These last eight days have been the happiest of my entire life, because we've been together. And for the past twenty-six years, our friendship has been my most fulfilling relationship of any kind."

My pulse raced, but I warned myself not to get my hopes up. "What are you saying?"

"I'm saying there's a reason that people have been assuming since we were teenagers that we're a couple. Everyone has always seen the love between us that we've claimed was platonic. But I realized today, it's not. I'm in love with you, and I'm pretty sure you're in love with me, too."

His words overjoyed me, and it was such a relief to hear I wasn't the only one who felt that way. But I still had to tease him a little. "You're *pretty* sure I'm in love with you, too? What's keeping you from believing that I'm stupid in love with you and probably have been since we were nine?" That night of his mom's car accident when I comforted him as he cried had imprinted on my heart a need to take care of him forever. It was only now I could admit to myself that it was love.

"I had to use the qualifier, because if I declared you were *definitely* in love with me, you'd accuse me of being a know-it-all smart-ass."

"You *are* a know-it-all smart-ass." I reached out

and pulled him into my embrace. "You also happen to be completely right, as always."

The beautiful smile he gave me lit me up inside, especially once he tugged on my suit jacket lapels to bring me down for a kiss. It was sweet and tender, filled with all our affection. I was stupid for ignoring my feelings for so long out of fear.

"You know what this means?"

"We get to go home, and I can make love to you instead of just fucking you into satisfied oblivion?" I asked in a hopeful voice.

"That, too. But it also means if I have to live with being your pookie for the rest of time, I get to come up with a pet name for you now."

The thought tickled me. "Oh, I'm in trouble, aren't I?"

"Considering how much trouble you get into, having my choice of calling you Julian, Jules, Julie, and a pet name seems like a fair way to handle it."

"Well, let's go back before I get us in trouble by going for round two in here." We savored another kiss before we held hands and started returning to the banquet hall. "I have to say, Rhys and Lucien have an incredible track record for getting friends to fall in love thanks to their weddings."

"They'll be delighted to hear it, despite Rhys assuming we've been together for years."

I grinned at the reminder. "I can't wait to visit you

in your office and have the kind of fun behind your closed door people assume we have."

"Don't get any ideas. We're not having sex in my office during business hours."

"What about after?"

He laughed as we entered the reception hall and headed back to our table, where all our family and friends were gathered, which now included Elias. He was animatedly talking with Callum, looking like a completely different person from earlier. It made me happy that we had all found what we needed.

Chapter Nine

XANDER

AFTER HAVING JOSH THROWN OUT, the wedding reception had become even more enjoyable. It was wonderful seeing Elias having an excellent time after the emotional roller coaster he had been on all day. I was proud of him for standing up for himself. We filled the night with fun and laughter.

It was almost two in the morning by the time we returned to Jules's apartment. I had very much been looking forward to being with Jules once we were home alone, but my exhaustion hit me hard when we entered his bedroom. I had been up since five to ensure every detail of Rhys's wedding had been perfect. It had been a long damn day.

All it took was one look into my tired eyes for him to press a soft kiss on my forehead and tell me, "It's late. Let's go to bed."

It didn't surprise me at all that he understood I

needed sleep more than sex. I hugged him in silent gratitude, sagging into the comfort of his warm embrace. He was the only person in the world who I was safe enough with to surrender to when I couldn't continue being strong on my own. Why had I wasted so many years looking for that comfort with other people?

"Are you indulging me with a lingering hug, or did you fall asleep standing up?"

"Not asleep." I cringed at how petulant I sounded, hiding my face against his chest. "Sorry."

Jules stepped back and began undressing me for bed. I shrugged out of my suit jacket when he pushed it off my shoulders, letting it drop to the floor. He removed my vest, tie, and shirt, before undoing the button and zipper of my slacks. "Underwear off or on?"

"Off." I appreciated him asking. "Sorry I'm ruining your fun with them."

"There's plenty of time for that later." He slid them down halfway. I didn't resist as he guided me to sit on his unmade bed. He untied my dress shoes, then took them and my socks off to allow him to remove my pants and underwear next.

My heart swelled with love when Jules hung my discarded outfit in his closet. "Thanks, Julie."

"You're welcome, pookie." He grinned as he stripped out of his clothes and put his suit on a hanger. If I wasn't there, it would be on the floor with the rest of the small pile of laundry at the foot of his bed. It meant a lot that he hung it up to avoid stressing me out about it getting wrinkled.

We took our turns in the bathroom, before he shut off the lights and joined me. I curled up beside him, relaxing when he wrapped his arms around me in a protective embrace. It would have been easy to drift off because of how tired I was, but it was important for me to mention something first. "I didn't say it earlier, but thank you for helping Elias."

"I'm glad I got there in time. I understand why you couldn't get mad at him for what Josh did. He's a good kid."

He really was. "I think Elias and Callum will become close friends after tonight."

"Yeah, I agree. It's amazing how much he's come out of his shell since being with my brother."

The first day I met Callum, he had been painfully shy but determined to be helpful to me. It took a few weeks before he could make small talk with me. Since being with Rune, he had grown more confident in himself. It showed with the way he had made Elias comfortable at our table after the showdown with Josh. "He's changed a lot, but he's still the same sweetheart he's always been. I'm so grateful to Rhys for hiring him. I wouldn't have survived this last-minute wedding prep without his help. He's also made an enormous difference in Rune, too. I've never seen him so happy and carefree in public before."

"I used to be so worried about him, but Callum turned my prickly hedgehog of a baby brother into a cute kitten."

The description amused me, but I could imagine Rune being annoyed by it. "You know he hates it when you refer to him as adorable animals."

"He also hated it when I told him he went from a sad little rain cloud to a fluffy cumulus one. That didn't stop me from teasing him about it. Besides, he got me back with years of snarky digs about me being in denial about you. Now, he gets to gloat about being right for the rest of my life, so we're more than even."

I frowned at his words. "How does that not bother you?"

"People have been saying shit like that to me forever, so I'm used to it. If anything, it'll be strange they can't bring it up now."

"No, I meant..."

Jules caressed me, soothing away my worries. "You can tell me."

I traced the ridge of his collarbone as I struggled to find the right words. "It bothers me that everyone assumed you were in love with me, but none of our friends thought I could reciprocate."

Jules squeezed my shoulder in comfort. "That's not true. They wouldn't have encouraged me to be honest if they believed I didn't stand a chance with you. Besides, every single one of your exes accused you of having feelings for me, so plenty of people thought you reciprocated my interest."

He wasn't wrong. That point of contention had led to quite a few of my breakups. How many times had I argued with absolute certainty that if I wanted Jules to be mine, he would be? How often had I claimed that I would be lucky to be loved by him? How had I never realized what it meant that I always chose him over my boyfriends? "I'm such an idiot."

"Hey, you're not allowed to be an idiot, because that would make me the biggest dumbass in history."

Guilt ate away at me. "At the very least, it makes me an enormous asshole."

Jules kissed my forehead. "You're not, so stop worrying."

My voice was barely louder than a whisper. "But I told so many of them you'd be mine if I wanted you."

"How does that make you an asshole when it was true?"

Sourness twisted in my gut. "I acted like if I snapped my fingers, you'd come running to be with me in an instant. That means all the years I wasted with other guys—"

Jules shifted our positions so I was on my back looking up at him. "That's not a road worth going down."

"But—"

He cut me off with a soft but demanding kiss. "No buts. None of that other stuff is important."

"It's my fault—"

"Don't play the blame game. If you do, I'm equally responsible here. Nothing good comes out of beating ourselves up for that."

He was right, but it didn't help lessen my remorse. "If I hadn't been so—"

Jules silenced me by placing his index finger over my lips. "Stop. Don't let past regrets steal your current happiness. It's not worth it."

"But—"

He talked over me. "Do you need me to show you why none of that matters now that we're together?"

"Please, Julie."

Despite my exhaustion, the kiss he gave me woke up my body. He touched me everywhere as he set about worshipping me. As he covered me with reverent kisses, he built my desire up to dizzying heights. I came alive under his teasing touches, aching for him. There was a slight possessiveness to his actions that drove me wild. I needed him to claim me as his and chase away any doubts I had.

His fingers drifted down to tease my hole. I attempted to draw him in, but he denied me. "Is this what you want?"

"Please!" The neediness in my voice should have embarrassed me, but I wanted him inside me too badly to be ashamed of my desire.

He reached over me to get lube and a condom from his nightstand, before stretching me with a patience I didn't have. I needed more than just fingers to satisfy me, but he distracted me with soft kisses. It was exquisite torture of the best kind.

My anticipation spiked when he withdrew. When he went to pick up the foil packet, I stopped him. "Make me yours, Julie."

His blue eyes burned with fiery passion as he asked in a dark growl, "What are you saying?"

My arousal intensified. "I want you to take me, with nothing in between us."

"Are you sure?"

I arched up underneath him, brushing my erection against his. "Yes!" While Josh and I had always used protection, I had gotten myself tested after I found out about his cheating. Thankfully, everything came out negative, so I wasn't putting Jules at risk.

He responded with a dominating kiss I surrendered to. I ran my fingers through his hair, trying to ground myself before his passion swept me away.

When we parted, I was breathless and aching for more. His chuckle sent a shudder through me as he rubbed his thumb over the head of my cock, smearing the precum that had gathered in my excitement. "You're practically dripping for me."

"I want you so much, *please*!"

As his hand retreated, I groaned with frustration. But that soon fled as he slicked his hardness with lube and pressed it against my entrance. It was a relief when he slid into me, but it surprised me how different it was when not using a condom. That thought didn't stick around for long once he started moving.

Instead of taking me hard and fast like I normally begged for, he went slow and gentle. He let his body tell me without words what I meant to him. Every thrust told me I was his as he showed me the difference between fucking and making love for the first time.

Our bodies rocked together, and I got lost in the rhythm. He murmured sweet words as he rolled his hips against me, his hands wandering to continue feathering light touches everywhere he could reach. It further heightened my pleasure as I basked in what it felt like to be treasured by Jules.

He hitched my left leg higher, allowing him to push deeper into me. It was incredible, especially once he moved with more force. My body grew taut when he took my hardness in hand. It was almost too much to bear. I teetered on the verge, needing a little more to take me over the edge.

"You're so beautiful, and you're *mine*." The possessiveness in his voice sent me soaring. "Even if I had to wait a thousand years to be with you like this, it would be worth it to love you."

"Julie!"

He leaned forward to kiss me, causing me to gasp at the shift in angles as he continued pleasuring me. I could only keen in response, too absorbed in the moment to say anything meaningful. It was easier to let my body whisper my secrets to him instead.

"I love you, pookie." With those words, he pushed all the way in and came with a moan.

My orgasm hit me so hard that my back bowed from the effort, a gasp getting caught in my throat. It left me trembling and oversensitive in its wake. I melted further when he kissed me. He was right; it wasn't worth wasting time on regrets when it felt so good to be his.

Chapter Ten

JULES

WHEN I WOKE UP, Xander was sitting propped up on the pillows next to me as he scrolled through his phone. It made me warm and fuzzy that he wanted to be near me, even when I was unconscious. I curled myself around him and slung my arm over his waist in a lazy half hug, mumbling some sounds that attempted to be a greeting.

"Morning."

I drifted somewhere between awake and asleep, enjoying the nearness of my best friend. When he snorted at something he read, it pulled my focus back to him. "Hmm?"

"Either this is a joke, or people are dumber than I thought."

With effort, I opened my eyes and blearily looked at his screen. "What's a 'face genius'?"

"According to this list, it's someone with a pretty

face." He shook his head. "I told you, these are so dumb. I'd never be able to call you 'Foo Foo' without blushing."

I had never been a morning person, so my mind was still sluggish from sleep. "Foo Foo?"

"Apparently, it's a guy who is overly extra. Who comes up with this nonsense? What poor bastard is getting called 'Foo Foo' because of his 'too much gene'?"

"Little Bunny Foo Foo?" It earned me a laugh from Xander. "Wait, are you looking up pet names for me?"

A slight flush graced his cheeks. "Yes, but there isn't anything on here that I could use in public. They're too stupid or embarrassing. 'Cuddles' would be appropriate, but I'd die of humiliation calling you that while we were out with people. I mean, cuddle bug? Cuddly wuddly? *Really?* And don't even get me started on all the muffins."

"Mm, muffins sound good."

"I can make you some, but I refuse to refer to you as 'Captain Love Muffin.'"

I howled with laughter. "*Captain Love Muffin?* What the hell is that?"

"They claim it's a boyfriend who loves to take charge. I call bullshit. But for some strange reason, there are thirteen names on here with 'muffin' in them. Why is it such a popular pet name?"

"Because they're sweet and people love to eat

them. And you're delicious, so I could eat you right up." I nipped at Xander's side, which resulted in a yelp of surprise before he swatted at me. "Maybe I should have stuck with calling you 'muffin' after all."

He pushed me backward, making me laugh. "Don't even think about it. Pookie is bad enough. Although, it's light-years better than most of what's on here. The only person who should be called 'monkey' is a rambunctious kid."

I mimicked a British accent as I joked, "Can I be your cheeky little monkey?"

He rolled his eyes, even as a smile tugged at his lips. "Seriously, who calls their beloved 'hidden crazy,' because 'he's a boyfriend who likes to be silly and have fun'? Can you imagine me talking with friends and saying, 'Yeah, hidden crazy and I had a wonderful anniversary at the vineyard last weekend,' without laughing?"

"It would be a misnomer in my case, since my crazy is usually on full display."

I delighted in his laughter. "Very true. Can you imagine? It would make me sound like I was dating brothers as boyfriends: hidden crazy and visible crazy. Not to mention having shitty taste in men."

"Yes, I think Rune and Callum would both have complaints if you tried to date me and my brother." I sat up and embraced him, resting my chin on his shoulder as I looked at his phone. "Honey bagel?

Honey smack? Honey sugar bumps? Who the hell made this list?"

He tapped the top of his screen to jump up to the beginning of the page. "The editorial team."

"That sounds ominous." My eyes went wide when I saw the article title. "*Twelve hundred plus* cute nicknames for boyfriends and their special meanings?"

He returned to where he was before. "Number three hundred and eighty-eight is 'hunk of man meat.' I don't hold out much hope for the rest of the list. Who in their right mind would ever say, 'Hey, hunk of man meat, would you please pass the salt?' This has to be a joke."

"Obviously, since they insist 'knee melter' is a thing."

"Huh, I didn't realize there was a technical term for all those times you've passionately kissed me and made me feel weak in the knees."

My ego purred at the compliment. "Maybe I'll add that to my business card. 'Professional graphic design artist and official knee melter.' That should earn me at least a few sales, right?"

"It beats the hell out of 'Lord of the Vikings' or 'love lumps.' I don't even like lumps in my mashed potatoes. Why would I call you that? Oh, and see? Love muffin! They add 'muffin' to everything."

He showed me on his phone as if I didn't believe him. "It makes me miss your chocolate chip muffins. It's been an eon since I got to enjoy those." I kissed his shoulder as I squeezed him tighter. Hugging him was the best feeling ever. "Do they really think someone will call their boyfriend 'love nugget' because 'he's your backbone'? I don't get it. What do backbones and boneless nuggets have to do with each other?"

"I have no clue. Wow, I was joking at the church about 'meatball' as a pet name, but it's actually on here."

"Too bad I'm disqualified since it specifies 'short men who are nutty.' Because I guess nothing says nutty like meatballs?"

Xander snickered. "Does that mean a 'meatloaf' is a tall guy who acts nuts? I wonder what the scale of meat-to-height ratio is of absurd nicknames?"

I laughed at the outlandish question. "No idea, but according to number five hundred and twenty-seven, I should start calling you 'Mister Bossy Pants' since you prefer to be in control."

"Do it, and you'll be 'Mister Monkey Muffins' for life."

He wasn't just being clever; it was entry five hundred and thirty-two. "Shit, you really weren't joking. They stuck 'muffin' on the end of *everything*." The one six below that had me grinning like a fool. "*Mookie-pookie bear?*" I fell against the pillows as I laughed so much I couldn't breathe.

"Yeah, yeah. Real fucking funny. This list says I can call you 'muffin head' affectionately since you've clearly lost your mind if you think you can address me as 'mookie-pookie bear' and live."

I finally got control of myself and sat up so I could stroke under his chin. "Aww, is my precious mookie-pookie bear mad?"

He knocked my hand away. "Okay, see, this bothers me. They say 'my Caesar' is a boyfriend 'who's your king.' But Caesar was a Roman emperor, not a king. That's insulting *and* inaccurate."

"It's hardly their most egregious error."

"I know I wouldn't be the only one bothered by it. Your brother and Callum both would already be halfway through writing an email telling them why they were wrong and needed to fix it."

"That's because they're both history nerds," I said with affection, before tacking on another suggested name, "my lil' chicken nugget."

He glared at me for that one. "I obviously need to start breakfast since you're hungry. Huh, look here. They claim I can call you 'numb nuts,' because it's 'a cute pet name for an amazing but dim-witted boyfriend.' Silly me, I always thought it was an insult."

"It's not as if this is the end all, be all of lists. They also say that 'pineapple chunk is a great nickname for an exotic boyfriend,' which seems offensive to me. Don't you agree, pookie wookie?" That one was on there, too.

Xander heaved a weary sigh. "I'm going to regret sharing this with you, aren't I?"

"Yeah, probably." I grinned at him. "Oh, that one's just nasty. Calling a guy 'rashes' because he's always on you? Ew."

"That's so gross." He shuddered in disgust as he scrolled down the page. "I swear to god, if you call me 'schmoopy pookie pooh,' I'll never have sex with you again."

The list continued to provide me with fun bastardizations of my pet name for Xander. "I sincerely doubt your ability to follow through on that threat."

He arched one of his perfect eyebrows at me. "You really want to try me? I'm used to long dry spells after being with Josh."

I kissed my way up Xander's neck, raising chills on his skin. When I reached his ear, I murmured, "Yes, but unlike him, I'm skilled at pleasuring you. You'll actually miss being satisfied by me."

Xander shied away from me, making me smirk. "Stop it. I'm perfectly capable of—*slut muffin*? How is *that* a term of endearment?"

I loved how easily that distracted him. "I don't know, spanky. Or should I call you 'spicy meatball' like number eight hundred and fifty-four suggests?"

He ignored me. "I'm amazed 'tiddlywinks' isn't on here. Or is that what 'tad winks' is supposed to be?

What the fuck is a tad winks? It's certainly not 'a boyfriend who comforts you.'"

"Got me. I'm still trying to figure out how 'thunder muffin' is considered romantic." As he continued browsing the absurd suggestions, another name jumped out at me. "An 'Uncle Upright is a boyfriend who always has a hard-on'? That sounds like bad porn."

"No 'tiddlywinks,' but they've got 'wink-a-dink' on here. What sense does that make?"

"Well, at least defining it as a guy who likes to fuck *kinda* makes sense. You know, if you squint at it, and suspend all disbelief." I couldn't get over how ridiculous the suggested names were. "Oh, so they'll stick 'wonder' in front of boy, guy, and man, but not muffin? I call shenanigans. And 'yes-guy' is an insult, not a nickname. Just because it's the casual form of 'yes-man,' doesn't mean it's romantic."

The list ended on "Zorro," which was disappointing. Xander locked his phone and tossed it aside on my nightstand in disgust. "Twelve hundred and forty-seven suggestions later, and I still don't have a good name for you. This sucks."

"In fairness, at least twelve hundred and thirty-eight of them were terrible."

He flopped onto the pillows with a huff. "I read three articles before that one, and none of them had anything appropriate for you. It shouldn't be this difficult to come up with a name."

It touched me he was taking something absurd so seriously. "I'm confident you'll figure it out."

Xander moved to straddle himself over my lap, pinning me against my pillow. My dick was immediately interested in where things seemed to be heading. "There's one thing that's bothering me more than that, though."

"Which is?"

"I've been too selfish." Before I could protest, he bent down and kissed me into silence. I opened for him, loving the feeling of our tongues teasing each other. I embraced him as he made me forget what he was talking about. "It's not fair I've taken all the pleasure."

"You say that like I haven't been enjoying myself. Being with you satisfies me in ways I hadn't known were possible."

He threw the covers off us, before covering me in kisses all over. His fingers toyed with my nipples until they hardened into nubs, before lapping at them with his tongue. I grew fully erect as he moved further south, trembling from the gentle brush of his long eyelashes against my skin. "It's your fault, you know. You're too good at giving me what I want."

"I fail to see how that's a bad thing." My breathing hitched when he took my hardness in hand and worked it. His pace was slow and deliberate, making me yearn for so much more than that. "*Please.*"

His green-hazel eyes were almost gold as they lit up with excitement. He made a show of lavishing oral attention on my balls as he stroked my length. I spread my legs further apart to give him better access, a sigh escaping from me as he continued.

It felt like forever until he licked his way up to my erection. He ran his tongue along the underside, before placing a teasing kiss on it with a hint of suction. I held my breath in anticipation, trembling as he gave me a taste of what was to come. He had me on the verge of begging for something more when he drew me into his mouth.

The slick heat was divine as he blew me, taking me deep and then backing off to just the tip. He drove me wild as he swallowed around me and moaned. It was surreal watching him going down on me, but it was also an enormous turn-on. He sucked my cock with the enthusiasm of someone who hadn't been able to enjoy doing so in a very long time. I wanted him to finish me, but if he did, it would mean it would be a while before I could take him how he liked. I figured the best way to get him to back off would be to annoy him. "Pookie, I'm too close—"

In response to the nickname, he applied the barest hint of teeth in displeasure. I surprised both of us when that made me come with a gasp. He swallowed with an amused expression. "Do you have a masochistic streak I don't know about?"

"I told you I was close. Let me return the favor."

He laughed as I flipped him over and pinned him under me. I started by trailing kisses up his length to the tip. To my surprise, he broke into a fit of giggles. "What?"

It took him a moment to regain his composure. "Sorry, you mentioned Little Bunny Foo Foo earlier, and seeing my cock bump against your lips made me think about that stupid song about bopping mice on the head."

"I'm sure you're more interested in me bobbing my head than bopping yours." To prove my point, I set about demonstrating the former as I took him into my mouth. He squirmed under me as I sucked him off, making delectable noises as he gripped one of my shoulders to ground himself. A few playful flicks of my tongue was all he needed to come. It was a much better start to my morning than a glass of orange juice.

He moaned in satisfaction, a sound I'd never get tired of inspiring. "You're a genius."

"I believe that article specified I'm a face genius, which I'm still not convinced is an actual thing."

Xander crooked his finger and gestured for me to come up to him. "C'mere, bunny."

I did as he wished but couldn't resist teasing, "Hey, that's Mr. Foo Foo to you."

"It's perfect. We go at it like rabbits, but you're cute like a bunny. It's the right mix of adorable and obnoxious."

"You know, I bet I could get famous if I made a webcomic about the adventures of Pookie and Bunny."

He laughed as he pulled me down for a kiss. For the first time, Xander cuddled me as I lay down on top of him with a contented sigh. While I loved being the one hugging, it was nice being held, too.

"That idea is definitely worth making you muffins."

"Excellent, I look forward to it later."

I could hear the smile in his voice. "Why am I not surprised you're choosing snuggling over food?"

"Because you've known me since we were eight."

Xander chuckled again as he tightened his arms around me. "For a cute bunny, you're a real smart-ass sometimes."

"Would you have me any other way?"

He kissed my forehead. "Nope, I'll take you as you are, sarcasm and all."

"That makes me the luckiest bunny in the world." It was by far the best lazy Sunday morning of my life being able to lounge in bed with him. I couldn't wait until every morning was like that for us. His delicious chocolate chip muffins would be a bonus.

Chapter Eleven
XANDER

AFTER A SEXY SHOWER, I baked chocolate chip muffins for breakfast. They had always been one of Jules's favorite things, but I discovered he had a new way of eating them. "Since when have you needed whipped cream for muffins?"

He responded by building a mountain out of it on his plate to use for dipping. "I bet people would be more willing to eat bran muffins if it came with a side of whipped cream." He tore off a piece and dunked it in the white peak. "You're seriously missing out."

"Somehow I doubt that."

Jules shrugged as he enjoyed a two-to-one ratio of whipped cream to muffin with every bite. "You're acting like it's weird."

"It *is* weird." I continued to savor mine without it. "Nobody eats muffins with whipped cream. How did this habit even get started?"

"I went to the Brewhaha Café where Rune met Callum. The barista knows I order extra whipped cream on my drinks, so Brinley gave me a side of it to go with my chocolate chip muffin one day."

"So, this woman hands you a plate of whipped cream for a *muffin* and you go, 'Yeah, that totally makes sense,' and dig in?"

He laughed as he added more to his plate for his second muffin. They never lasted long around him. "No, I asked her why, and she said she assumed I liked whipped cream with everything."

I snorted at that. "There's not a chance in hell you didn't snicker and make her think you're into using it with sex."

Jules flashed a cheeky grin, making me laugh. "You would be correct, sir. Brinley then blushed and told me her favorite food was chocolate chip pancakes with whipped cream, so she eats her chocolate chip muffins the same way. I informed her she was a genius, then enjoyed the hell out of that muffin."

"And probably licked the damn plate when you finished." It wouldn't be the first time Jules had done such a thing.

"Hey, give me a *little* credit. I was in public."

I scoffed at his claim. "Since when has that stopped you? If I recall correctly, you ended up dating Nick after he saw you lick whipped cream off my finger at the diner we went to during college."

"That was because his mind jumped straight from

that to blow jobs, which was exactly what I was trying to make him think of." Jules smirked as I tried not to get distracted by our morning starting that way. "I pity whoever he ended up with. All he wanted to do was fight, and he was terrible in bed."

"We should look him up and give him Josh's number. They'd be a match made in Hell." My own joke amused me, but the subject caused me to belatedly realize something. "Huh, you've never really had a type."

"Wow, that's quite the transition." He finished his muffin, then used his finger to finish the last bit of whipped cream. "What brought that up?"

I thought back to some of Jules's previous boyfriends compared to my own. "I've always dated older guys, because they tend to have their shit together more than people my own age. Most of them have been on the more serious side personality-wise, and they've all been tops. But none of your exes have much in common with each other."

He shrugged. "You know me. I'm the curious type."

"I'd say. You went from average Nick, to professional bodybuilder Dwayne who could deadlift you with one pinky, then your boyfriend after that was a twink. I never understood that."

"Why I dated Micah after Dwayne?"

I nodded. "Dwayne was always the big question

mark for me. He didn't fit with any of the other guys you had been with." The guy had been massive, with the biggest muscles I had ever seen in real life. He looked like a stereotypical asshole gym rat, but he had been a gentle giant and an eighth-grade math teacher. The only reason they broke up was because Dwayne had to move back to the East Coast to take care of his sick parents. He was the poster boy for never judge a book by its cover.

"Yes, but he was also kind, caring, and generous, which were all the total opposite of Nick. He gave killer bear hugs. Why is that odd?"

"It's because he didn't seem like—" I cut myself off when I realized what I almost said.

"He didn't seem like what?"

I cursed myself for accidentally setting a trap for myself. "No, it's not my place to judge."

Jules rested his elbow on the table and propped his chin on his hand as he studied me. "Now I have to know."

"You really don't."

"If you don't tell me, I'll start guessing. I have a whole new arsenal of methods to extract a confession out of you, so keep that in mind."

Dancing around the issue would turn it into a bigger deal than it was, so I sucked up my embarrassment and finished my sentence. "He didn't seem like a typical bottom."

Jules cracked up into peals of laughter. It took him

a few moments to regain control of himself. "You're too funny."

"Why does that make me funny?"

"He didn't seem like a typical bottom because he wasn't one."

"I was unaware that an atypical bottom was a thing."

My question set off another round of giggles in Jules. "Stop, stop, I can't take it anymore!" He was gasping for air as he wiped away tears from his eyes. "You're killing me! That would be like a Chihuahua trying to top a Great Dane!"

I had to snicker at his description. At the same time, it also left me with an uncomfortable jealousy, knowing they had only broken up because of Dwayne's move. If he hadn't gone home to his family, would they have stayed together? I *really* didn't like the thought of that.

He finally regained his composure before he responded, "You only date guys like him for one reason: to have him drill you into the mattress with all that muscle. He was a thousand percent a top."

I stared at Jules, who was so good at taking control of me and being the dominant partner in our encounters. The situation became a lot less funny when I realized my selfishness might have been worse than I thought. How had it never occurred to me that maybe he wanted it the other way around? I was such an idiot.

Intuitive as ever, Jules turned serious. He got up and took my hand to lead me over to the couch so we could sit next to each other. "Before you beat yourself up, remember that I went from Dwayne to Micah for a reason. I missed being the one giving pleasure."

"But the inverse of that is you miss receiving it." His hesitation to answer made it worse. "Shit, I've been so selfish and—"

Jules took my face between his hands and shushed me. "Nope, I'm not letting you beat yourself up over this. There's no need. Listen to me, Xander. I have never in my life been so happy or so satisfied. It's not about who's on top or bottom. It's about being with *you*. That's what makes me feel best."

"Can you honestly sit there and tell me you're fine that it's been so one-sided?"

"It hasn't been, unless you're not enjoying yourself. But based on the sounds you make, I'm doing a damn good job of ensuring you're having fun, so I don't buy that."

I held his wrists but didn't move his hands away from my face. "Be honest with me, Julian."

He frowned, brushing my cheeks with thumbs to comfort both of us. "I *am* being honest. What do I have to do to make you believe that I've enjoyed every second of being with you and wouldn't change a single thing?"

"Yeah, but…"

Jules sat back, making me mourn the loss of his

touch. "Look, you can take my word for it, or I can be blunt with you if that's what you need to hear. No bullshit, just brutal honesty."

I braced myself for what was about to happen. "Tell me."

He took a moment to sort out his thoughts, which made my nerves fray at the edges. "Please understand I'm saying this with all the love in my heart, but you're a perfectionist who needs to maintain control at all times for a sense of security."

How could I get offended when it was true? "You're not wrong."

"When your world is caving in, when nothing is going right, or when you're on the verge of losing it, what do you do?"

There was no need to think about that answer. "I go to you."

"Exactly. I understand what it means for you to share your burdens with me. You know I'll always take care of you, that I'd do anything to protect you. That was true when we were kids, when we were just friends, and when we're together. Agree or disagree?"

"Agree."

"Good. In the past, that meant I would hug you or make you laugh. Now, I have other options at my disposal to help you feel better."

I smirked. "You make me feel more than better."

"Yeah, I do." He looked pleased with himself, before turning serious once more. "To enjoy pleasure without ruining it with thinking, you have to let go of all your problems, your concerns, your control. You need pushed to your limits to get you to that point. Aggressive fucking is *very* effective at that. Especially because you know you'll be safe when you surrender to me."

The thought sent a shiver down my spine. "You've become quite an expert at knowing how far to take it."

"Doing that is sexy, and exhilarating, and a million other wonderful things. I also understand that you had a *lot* of aggression you needed to work through because of your situation with Josh."

"But?"

He took a deep breath before confessing. "But sometimes I worry I'm taking it too far or that I might hurt you. I wish I could be more gentle with you and take my time in pleasuring every inch of you. But you weren't in a place where that was what you wanted or needed. I get that. I'm not judging you for it at all, because I understand."

"I'm sor—"

"You don't need to apologize when you've done nothing wrong."

It was a challenge, but I swallowed the rest of my apology. "I didn't mean to be selfish. You're just so good at giving me what I wanted, I didn't think you'd want things to be different."

"I very much enjoy taking the lead most of the

time, but sometimes it's nice to embrace someone with your entire body. It's the ultimate hug for me." As if sensing the road my thoughts were heading down, Jules gave me a stern look. "Stop it. Don't twist my words to make yourself feel bad. If it was what I wanted, I would have asked."

That was an excellent point. He had never been shy about making his wants known. But I couldn't shake the awful guilt for denying that kind of hug when I knew how much he enjoyed them.

"Obviously, I need to take some drastic measures to get you out of your head on this issue." He took a deep breath. "Brace yourself, because I'm about to say some really embarrassing shit that I'll deny I ever said after this conversation is over."

Despite the plunge in my mood, it piqued my curiosity. "Like what?"

"I enjoy indulging you when you're selfish. I think you're adorable when you get demanding. I fucking love it when you boss me around. If you barge into my apartment unannounced and command me to shut up and hug you again, I won't be able to do it without getting a hard-on. That's how much your authoritative streak arouses me."

He was right. That was all information he *definitely* shouldn't have told me, because I would one hundred percent use it to my advantage later. "Why?"

"Because I'm the only person who *ever* sees you like that. With everyone else, you're a flawless, untouchable beauty who can do no wrong. But I'm lucky enough to enjoy watching your beautiful lips pout and get to entertain you in your rare petulant moments. I appreciate your absolute faith in me that I'll obey any of your whims."

His words took me aback. "It's not like I go, 'Hm, work was a disaster today, so I'll go bark orders at Jules to feel better.' I'm not—"

He interrupted me by pulling me into his lap. "Don't get defensive about something I'm telling you I enjoy."

"But it makes me sound like a massive asshole!"

He chuckled, disarming some of my uneasiness. "No, what that tells me is your trust in me is so deeply engrained that you do it without thinking. I treasure that, because you are not a man who easily trusts."

It humored him, but all I could see were the problems. Because I had felt completely out of control at work and because of my situation with Josh, I had gone to Jules. I had forced him to cuddle with me, agree to attend the wedding as my fake date, and then suggested we be friends-with-benefits. Afterward, I had told him we were in love. The realization made me ill. "How do you not hate me?"

"There's nothing you could do that would ever make me hate you. Stop telling yourself that you manipulated me into being with you, because it's not even remotely true."

He really knew me too well. "But—"

"Xander, I'm many things, but a doormat isn't one of them. If I was uncomfortable with something you asked me to do, I would tell you. Yes, you ordered me to hug you, but you know damn well that's my favorite thing in the world. Yes, you demanded I get in bed with you, but on what planet would I turn down the rare opportunity to cuddle with you? It's horizontal hugging at its finest."

He had always been a master at getting me to laugh no matter what. "I guess."

"See, the thing is, I told you I had a dream about you and your underwear that night. What I didn't tell you is I came from it because you moaned my name in your sleep while caressing me."

I blinked at him. "I'm sorry, I did what now?"

"You had slipped your hand under my shirt at some point during the night. When I jolted awake, you caressed my stomach as you mumbled 'Julie,' and I came in my underwear like a goddamn teenager. Not only that, but I stayed like that, because that's how much I couldn't bear to let you go when you were finally in my arms."

His blush went a long way toward making me feel better. "Seriously?"

"That entire breakfast, I kept wondering if I was right about your underwear. I couldn't get more coffee, because then you would have seen I was erect from thinking about you in my shower. Why do you think I dragged you back to my bedroom like a horny caveman as soon as I realized you were serious about hooking up? My dick wasn't as hard as a diamond because I was obligated to have sex with you since that's what you wanted. I wanted it, too. *Desperately*."

"Okay, before we both get too distracted, we'll put a pin in that and come back to it later." I couldn't figure out a smooth way to say what I needed to know, so I forced myself to ask the awkward thing. "Do you want me to fuck you?"

He burst into laughter, causing me to scowl.

"I'm being serious, Julian!"

Jules reined in his amusement. "Would I get off on you ordering me around in the bedroom? Absolutely. That's true regardless of who's on top. Do I think you would enjoy absolute control over me in that situation? Yes, once you quit worrying about if you were doing a good job or not. Do I want you to do that if you aren't comfortable with it? Absolutely not. Do I need you to do that to be happy? Not at all. In case it's not blindingly obvious, the thing I love the most is giving you pleasure, regardless of the form it takes."

"But do you—do you ever have days when you wish I would…" I lost my nerve to finish my sentence.

He did a shitty job of concealing his amused grin. "Wish you would pound me into the mattress?"

The heat on my cheeks crept up my neck to my ears. "Yeah."

"No, I don't. There's a reason I only dated one guy like Dwayne." My confusion must have shown on my face, because he bit his lip to hold in another laugh. "Physical domination isn't my thing. Wishing you would be a complete bastard and tease me until I lose my mind? That's a completely different story."

"Are you saying you want me to be a cocktease?"

"I'm going to regret asking for this, aren't I?" He looked more entertained by the prospect than scared.

I couldn't see myself physically dominating Jules, but toying with him was something else altogether. It was an art form I mastered from a very young age with him. "Your reaction to my blow job earlier suddenly makes a hell of a lot more sense."

"How is it news to you I like it when you're capricious? It keeps things interesting."

The potential for fun overruled my reservations. "You've intrigued me."

Interest sparked in his blue eyes. "Have I?"

I wrapped my arms around his neck in a loose hold. "I'm curious to see if you enjoy me being bossy and coy as much as you claim." The hardness springing up between us gave me a clue about how into the idea he was.

"Just say the magic words."

"Let's go play, bunny." It still felt strange calling him by a pet name, but it also was kind of fitting.

He swept me up to carry me back to his bedroom. I clung to him with a laugh, curious about what came next. "Seems like somebody's eager."

"Oh, you have no idea." He lowered me to stand

near the bed, allowing me to see the very visible tent in his pants at the prospect of being ordered around by me.

Knowing that I affected him to that degree gave me a thrilling rush. Since I was supposed to take the lead, I wasn't sure what else I could say other than order, "Strip."

He pulled off his yellow shirt, throwing it on top of his pile of clothes on the floor. Ever the show-off, he turned around as he lowered his red pajama bottoms, which were covered in bowls filled with ramen noodles that said "Send Noods." He glanced at me over his shoulder with a cheeky grin. Inch by inch, he revealed his bare ass, before kicking the pants and his briefs aside. His performance made me hard as a rock.

The view also caused me to realize how little I had taken the time to appreciate Jules's physique since our friendship had turned romantic. He had a swimmer's build, with a lean frame and muscles toned from years of karate practice. I couldn't resist letting my hands trail down his back to give his cheeks a gentle squeeze. "Is it weird I almost feel like I owe your ass an apology for ignoring it when it's this perfect?"

He turned to smirk at me. "Feel free to kiss it and make it better."

"I'll pretend you didn't just tell me to kiss your ass." Refocusing my attention, I hugged him from behind, but I was about two inches shy of being able to rest my chin on his shoulder. "This is…"

"Not quite right?"

That was my exact issue. "You're too tall to be the little spoon."

"Maybe you're too short to be the big spoon. Did you ever think of that?"

I tweaked one of his nipples as punishment for the comment.

He scoffed at my form of payback. "If that was your attempt at a purple nurple, it was pathetic."

"*Purple nurple*? What are you, twelve?"

Jules guided my right hand down to wrap around his erection. "Does this feel like I'm twelve?"

I couldn't resist the punchline. "Actually, this feels more like nine to me."

"You're *literally* stroking my ego. All eight inches of it."

I kissed my way up his neck. "Trust me, my ass knows it's nine."

"Huh, I didn't realize the stick up your ass was a ruler."

It was hard not to laugh. "Instead of being such a smart aleck, why don't you make yourself useful and take off my clothes?"

He turned around with a sexy smirk. "Should I say, 'Yes, sir,' while I'm at it?"

I remembered earlier he said he liked it when I got

authoritative with him, so I figured it was worth a shot. "Absolutely."

He grabbed the front of my shirt and roughly tugged me against him. "As you wish, *sir*." The word "sir" came out as a sensuous rumble, which sent shivers down my spine. He then kissed me hard, making me hold on to him before I lost myself to desire. His tongue explored my mouth, teasing mine as he made me weak in the knees.

It took effort to pull back from him, but I found the strength in me somehow. "I told you to undress me, not kiss me."

"My apologies, sir." He didn't look repentant at all as he stripped off my clothes. "Do you want me to make it up to you?"

I recognized he was giving me an out with his question, in case I had changed my mind about being top. Offering me a way to bail without asking was such a Jules thing to do. But I wasn't ready to give up control yet. "You can start by getting on the bed."

Never one to simply do as he was told, he crawled onto his sheets on all fours after pulling back the comforter. He then stretched out his arms in front of him as he rested on his knees, his ass up in the air. It was quite the position. His voice was a silken purr as he asked, "Is this how you want me, sir?"

I knelt behind him, enjoying the spectacular view. It gave me a better appreciation for why my partners enjoyed me from that angle. The temptation to reach out and touch was too much, so I fondled his pert ass as I considered my options. "For now."

To get the lube, I had to move. I walked over to his nightstand where he kept it during our early encounters. My eyebrows arched up at what I found in the top drawer. It was a chaotic mess of colorful dildos, cock rings, anal beads, and other sex toys strewn about, some of which I didn't even understand how they worked. "I guess that answers why you were fine being single these past few years."

Jules lacked any sense of shame, which was something I loved about him. "It keeps me entertained."

I pulled out an almost fifteen-inch doubled-ended clear purple dildo and held it up to him. "Do I even want to know?"

"Ty forgot to take it with him."

I stared at him in disbelief. "You dated him five years ago!"

"So? It's my junk drawer."

I snorted in amusement. Given the number of dildos in there, it was a great pun. I traded what was in my hand for a pair of pink fuzzy handcuffs. "And these?"

"Angelo had a sense of humor. There's heart-shaped keys for them in there somewhere." He sighed as I continued poking through his nightstand. "Are you looking for something to use, or are you trying to organize it?"

I grabbed the bottle and shut the drawer. "Fine, we'll go through it later."

"Are you planning on organizing them by type and color, or are you going to do it alphabetically? I bet you already have a spreadsheet planned out in your mind to keep track of them in the future."

"Ha ha, very funny." I flipped open the cap on the bottle and squirted out some cool gel. It was strange being on this side of things for the first time. "Ready?"

I could hear the grin in his voice as he answered, "Yes, sir."

With slight trepidation, I spread his cheeks to reveal his pucker, then slid in a single finger. The squelching of the lube as I moved made my own ass ache for Jules, but I focused on my task. It fascinated me to see part of myself moving in and out of my best friend in such an intimate way.

"Sir, I can handle more."

I took the passive-aggressive hint for what it was, adding a second finger inside him. He shifted on his knees as he pushed back against me with a satisfied sigh. It made me wonder about his experiences. "How long has it been for you?"

"Since I've had fingers in my ass, or since I bottomed?"

If he was offering, I intended to accept. "Both."

"Fingers was probably a few months ago? For

bottoming, it's been—I don't know, maybe about three or four years?"

I wasn't sure which number surprised me more. "Months?"

"Why are you shocked by that after seeing my junk drawer?"

"Because I can't imagine not using my fingers to get myself off for *months*."

He pushed back hard against me, which I took as a silent indicator he wanted more. I obliged him with a third finger, watching with interest as his hole spread to accommodate me. It was a huge turn-on for me. I almost missed him saying, "It's more of an occasional thing than a regular urge."

The answer was unexpected. "How often is occasionally?"

"Are you worried you'll have to fight me for the bottom?"

"Maybe?" I wasn't entirely sure.

"You have nothing to worry about, sir. Anytime you want to top, tell me. When I want to bottom, I'll let you know. I won't make you play a guessing game."

After all the mind games Josh played with me, it was such a relief to not have to deal with that. "But playing Questions with you is so much fun."

"I can think of something else that's *much* more fun."

It wasn't hard to decipher that clue. I withdrew

my fingers but had nothing to wipe them off with. In my excitement, I had forgotten to grab a towel like normal.

"Use the sheets." It came as no surprise he knew where my brain went.

"Absolutely not!"

"I'll do laundry later. It's not like water-soluble lube stains." He laughed when I got up to grab a towel from his bathroom closet. "Why do I get the feeling you're about to whip my ass like we're in a high school locker room?"

The thought had crossed my mind, but I remembered he said earlier he didn't enjoy physical domination the way I did. I settled for wiping my hand clean. "On your back."

That was one command he was eager to obey. He spread his legs wider so I could kneel between them and lean forward to brace myself on the bed over him.

I bent down for a soft, teasing kiss. He reached up to stroke my hair, and I leaned into his touch before I moved down his neck. While I had played a little earlier that morning, I took my time as I caressed him all over while I explored with my lips. I wasn't the best with words, but I wanted Jules to understand without a doubt how much I treasured him. He always did so much for me, and I was eager to return the favor.

That's why I kissed each mole and mark on him. I knew the history behind every scar, because I had been there for all of it. Nobody else he had been with was aware the bump on his collarbone was from breaking it falling out of the top bunk when we were kids. They probably didn't even notice it was there at all since it was so small. I was familiar with all the secrets of his body except for one, which I was about to uncover.

"Is this you playing coy, or are you stalling?"

"Maybe a little of both." My heart pounded as I used some lube to slick my cock up to prepare for what I was about to do.

Jules shifted his hips up in silent offering. I pulled him closer, before pushing into him. It had been one thing to experience his tight heat with my fingers; it was something else entirely when his body squeezed me on the most intimate level. I was so captivated that I reverently whispered his pet name without thought. "*Bunny*." Despite how amazing it felt, I still wiped my hand clean on the towel so I could touch him without making a mess.

"That's it. Nice and easy, pookie."

The occasion was too special to keep playing the "sir" game, so I didn't correct him. I appreciated his encouragement as I slid deeper into him, needing to adjust almost as much as him. To steady myself, I held on to his thighs as I tried to gather my bearings. When he tightened his muscles around me, I pushed into the sensation. "Sorry, I—"

"Don't apologize; do it again. And again, and

again, and again." He grinned at me, his teasing setting me at ease.

That was the permission I needed. I started off with tentative movements as I got used to being the one penetrating my partner. His tight heat surrounding me was beyond incredible, but it didn't take long before my perfectionism kicked in to question if I was doing it right. I didn't want to screw up and disappoint Jules after he had opened up to me about his desires.

He reached up and pulled me down to be closer to him. The shift in angles made him gasp, but I heard the pleasure in it. "Stop worrying about being perfect. This is just me and you, feeling good together."

Jules was right. He would never judge me, even if I did a horrible job. There was no place for doubts with us. I was with the only person I could relax and let my guard down in front of, who didn't expect me to be anyone other than my real self. He was the person who loved me the most in the entire world. Nothing I did would ever change that. He was mine, and I was his. The pleasure would be better because we'd experience it together. I surrendered myself to him completely and started chasing the sensations between us.

Chapter Twelve

JULES

ONCE XANDER SURRENDERED to the pleasure, the good turned to incredible. Given his tastes, I had expected him to establish a harsher rhythm once he grew comfortable. But his gentleness surprised me. I welcomed him deeper, savoring being so connected with my best friend. That was the closeness I craved above all else. I wrapped my legs around his waist and looped my arms over his neck to embrace him intimately on every level. I loved hugging and sex, which was why hugging with my entire body during sex was the ultimate experience for me. It allowed me to get as close as was physically possible.

Our friendship made the bond between us even more powerful. The few people I had bottomed with before had been enjoyable experiences, but nothing compared to feeling like I was part of Xander as we moved together as one.

I was awash in pleasure, lost in my love for my best friend, who was so much more to me than I ever thought would be allowed. After years of swallowing down the burning acid of jealousy, he was finally mine. It was so freeing to stop pretending not to notice my feelings for him anymore. I was flying high, with every pump of his hips sending me soaring.

When I told him I wished he'd tease the hell out of me, I hadn't been lying. It was something I looked forward to later, once he built up his confidence in taking the lead. But having him make love to me while looking at me with affection, that was what I craved most.

I gasped when he shifted angles, setting off a firework explosion inside me as he went deeper than before. To ground myself, I laced my fingers through his hair. I forgot how to breathe, think, or do anything other than feel. As much as I wanted to give him positive reinforcement by telling him how well he was doing, words were beyond me. It was everything I could do just to hold on and experience the toe-curling satisfaction.

Resisting the urge to touch myself and make it even better was challenging. However, Xander had a difficult time accepting my reassurance sometimes. Giving him hard evidence would be more convincing. As he moved with more vigor, it wouldn't be long for either of us.

"*Julie.*" He whispered it like it was the most sacred

word in the English language. I had taken a lot of shit about having a girly nickname from our mutual friends growing up, but I never gave a single fuck about what they thought. It meant more to me that it was a special name he used in those moments when he felt closest to me.

My muscles tensed as I neared my orgasm. All I needed was a little more to take me over the edge. Hearing him moan "Bunny" was what did it for me, because it was the word that let me into the parts of his heart nobody else would ever be allowed to see.

I came as I called out, "Pookie!" Yes, it was a silly name, but it held so much meaning because I was the only one who could get away with using it for him.

It only took a few more thrusts before he followed suit, pushing in deep and coming with a gasp. We remained still as we gathered our bearings. It didn't surprise me at all when his doubt kicked in almost immediately. "Was that terrible? Did I—"

I knew better than to let him finish his question. Our years of friendship had taught me that the best method to distract him from his anxiety was to confuse him. "Where are my hands?"

"Huh?"

"Where are my hands?" I caressed his hair with my right hand and brushed my left thumb against the back of his neck as a hint.

"Why are you—"

I interrupted him again. "Where are *your* hands?"

His fingers reflexively tightened on my hips he was still possessively holding, his gaze lingering on my cum-covered stomach. It took a second for the dots to connect for him, but his surprised reaction was priceless. "*Oh.*"

"Does that answer your question?"

"Uh, yeah, I guess that does." His pleased smile was precious, so I guided him closer for a kiss that would further convince him I was deeply satisfied.

It was hard not to groan at the sudden emptiness when he pulled out of me. I held my arms open to Xander, and he was all too happy to lie on top of me for another hug. Holding him tight, I reassured him further. "It was so perfect that I couldn't form the words to tell you how amazing it was. You have nothing to worry about. That was *incredible.*"

"Even though I got so caught up in the moment I forgot I was supposed to be teasing you?"

I rubbed his back to soothe away his concerns. "There's plenty of time for that later. You gave me exactly what I wanted, which was to be close to you."

"And to hug me like an octopus?"

There was no point in denying what was true. "That was one of my favorite parts."

"I'm sorry. I should have thought of that sooner." He sighed in disappointment at himself. "I don't know how I missed something so obvious."

"Again, if it had been a priority for me, I would have told you," I reminded him. "You have absolutely nothing to feel bad about. I'm covered in evidence of how much I enjoyed myself."

"You mean *we're* covered in it." We both chuckled at that, but he tensed up from a realization. "Oh, I should have cleaned—"

I shushed him. "Relax. You're right where I want you. I'm not ready to let you go yet."

"But you're always so good with aftercare, and—"

"That's because you hate messes. As my floor hamper shows, I'm fine with leaving things where they are. It gives us an excuse to take a sexy shower later, so stop worrying."

My comment did what I had hoped it would do; it made him snicker. "*Floor hamper?* Is that what you're calling it now?"

"As you know, I've been a firm believer for many years that a floor is a shelf for everything."

"Oh, trust me. I am *well* aware of that."

He should be, considering he had been in every single bedroom I had ever had since I was eight. "The flooring at the foot of my bed specializes in doubling as a hamper. And I didn't have to pay extra for it!"

He laughed, finally relaxing as his doubts subsided. "I should've started calling you 'bunny' years ago. It's like you're trying to make your own burrow out of dirty clothes."

"It would only be a problem if I never washed them. I'm perfectly capable of doing my laundry, thank you."

"Speaking of washing…"

I chuckled at the segue. "I'll never say no to a shower with you. You first."

Before he rolled off me, Xander propped himself up to look down at me. The adoration I saw in his green-hazel eyes was beautiful. "I love you, dirty clothes and all."

"I love you just as much, even when you're reorganizing my junk drawer later." He never could resist a project.

That got a big laugh out of him. "Come on, bunny. Let's go hop in the shower."

I couldn't think of a better way to spend an afternoon.

Chapter Thirteen

XANDER

RHYS HAD GIVEN both me and Callum three weeks off while he was on his second honeymoon. While appreciated, the workaholic in me was incapable of taking off that much time. When no one expected me to be in, it was the perfect chance to get some stuff done without being disturbed.

I waited until almost eight at night to go into work the Monday after the wedding, since everyone should be gone by then. My floor was empty as I headed toward my office, but I noticed someone behind Callum's reception-style desk. "Elias?"

He startled at the sound of his name, turning around to face me. "Xander? What are you doing here? I thought you were on vacation."

"I am. What are you doing here so late?"

"Dad forgot some files here for his meeting

tomorrow morning. Since I was at a nearby restaurant having dinner, I offered to come pick them up."

That explained why he was in the office, but not why he was behind my personal assistant's desk when he worked on a different floor. It also reminded me I forgot to grab something to eat before coming in. *Damn it.* "Did you need something here?"

"No, I was leaving this for Callum when he gets back." He held up a small, white envelope, before placing it on Callum's chair. "Um, I also have one for you and Jules, if that's okay."

I gestured for him to follow me into my office. Turning on my lights, I took a seat behind my desk as he sat before me once more. It was amazing what a difference a week made in how I reacted to him being in my space.

He passed over two envelopes identical to the one he had left for Callum. His penmanship was impeccable. "If you could give Jules his, I'd appreciate it."

"Sure. Should I read mine now?"

Elias shook his head. "Oh, please don't. It would be too embarrassing."

"Why?"

He nervously smoothed the hair at the nape of his neck. "I know it's weird a guy my age writes thank-you cards."

"All it means is that you had a thoughtful mother who taught you proper manners."

A slight smile graced Elias's lips. "I used to hate

when she insisted I had to write notes to people. But she was a firm believer in never wasting anyone's kindness with ingratitude. She insisted thank-you cards were powerful because no one ever expected them. It wasn't until she—"

When he cut himself off, I prompted him, "Until she what?"

"Never mind. I'm sure that's more detail about my personal life than you'd be interested in hearing."

That would be true normally, but I was in a generous mood. "If you feel like sharing, I'm curious."

He looked at me as if he didn't quite believe I was serious, before dropping his gaze to his hands in his lap. "It was only after she got sick that I understood how important thank-you cards could be. When she was diagnosed with cancer, I felt so helpless, like there wasn't anything I could do to make things better."

Based on the fact he had only referred to her in the past tense, I got the impression the story didn't have a happy ending. "I'm so sorry, Elias. That must have been awful to go through."

"Yeah." He rubbed the back of his hand, still not able to look up at me. "But I realized there was at least one thing that I could do to bring a smile to her face. I started writing her thank-you cards every day. Sometimes I'd thank her for something she did for me the day before. A lot of times, it was for small things she did for me growing up that I was too young to fully appreciate back then, like reading to me every night when I was a kid and teaching me to love books."

"She must have loved that."

Elias's gray eyes grew glassy with unshed tears. "She really did. Mom kept all of them and would read them on the bad days to help make herself feel better. It wasn't much, but it was something. And at least she knew without a doubt that I was grateful to have the best mother ever."

His story touched me. It was such a far cry from my relationship with my own mother, that I almost couldn't fathom it. "I think that's sweet that you did that for her."

"What I didn't find out until she passed away in January was that she had been writing me thank-you cards all along and saving them for me." He wiped the tears that had gathered in the corner of his eyes. "She kept them all in an organized box for me, with ones for birthdays, when I meet someone special, get engaged, married, all the major milestones. But most of them are random thank-yous for being her son and all those little moments that meant so much to her. I save those for days where I really need them, so I always have something to look forward to."

Poor Elias. I couldn't imagine losing a parent who would do that kind of thing for their child. My own mother would never do such a thing for me. "I'm so glad you have that. What an amazing gift."

He wiped away his tears again before they could fall. "You know, it's funny. In her own way, she tried to warn me about Josh. Because I didn't open her card about when I meet the man I want to spend the rest of my life with. I think I knew on a subconscious level that he wasn't worthy of her kind words. But after she passed two months ago, I was so lost. Dad grew more distant as he threw himself into work, so I was all alone. I just wanted somebody to love me again, so when Josh approached me after her funeral, I…"

"Oh, Elias, I'm so sorry." I wasn't sure what else I could say to his heartbreaking admission. "It'll happen, I promise. Don't let that asshole convince you otherwise."

"Thanks." His smile was a little sad, making me feel worse for him. "After seeing you and Jules, plus Callum and Rune, I get it now. A relationship with someone like that is who my mom's card is meant for."

"It's hard to be alone sometimes, but you don't have to settle. Especially not for somebody like Josh. You deserve so much more than that."

"You're right." He sat up a little straighter in the chair. "Anyway, I appreciate you listening. That was probably uncomfortable to hear, but—"

I gently interrupted him. "No, that was a beautiful story. I'm glad you shared that with me."

"Writing Mom a daily note had become a ritual for me, so when I couldn't do that anymore, it's part of why I felt so lost. I considered doing them anyway, but knowing she wasn't there to read them hurt too much. But thanks to the three of you, I had a reason to be thankful again. Being able to write the cards comforted me. It sounds strange, but it was very healing."

"It's a way of carrying on your mom's legacy of kindness."

"Exactly." His expression changed as he remembered something. "Oh, you probably didn't hear the news yet."

I couldn't tell if it was a good thing or a bad thing based on his tone. "News?"

"About Josh."

I held in a groan. "What did he do now?"

"He got fired today."

"*What?*" My brain boggled at the information. "What happened?"

"Um, well—I'm not sure how to tell you this, but it turns out that Josh had also been cheating on us with Henry."

After the past few weeks, nothing surprised me anymore. I tried to remember who Henry was but drew a blank. "Sorry, who's Henry?"

"I'm not sure if you know him. He's the person in charge of recording our billable hours. Josh accessed the reporting program through Henry's computer at his apartment and secretly increased his hours, hoping it would help him get promoted. Henry caught him doing it Saturday night after he went there to stay when I kicked him out."

It wasn't professional, but the information merited me saying, "Wow, he really is that stupid."

"Oh, it gets—well, worse or better depending on your stance, I guess. They had a nasty fight, so neighbors called the police. Josh got into it with the cops and ended up getting arrested. Between forging his hours and being charged with disorderly conduct and assaulting an officer, Dad had ample reasons to fire Josh when he came in this morning acting like nothing had happened."

I had to hide my inappropriate grin behind my hand. It served the bastard right to lose everything because of being a lying, cheating dick. "I'm glad your father handled the situation. It's what Josh deserves. Henry wasn't in trouble, was he?"

Despite no one being around, Elias lowered his voice so as not to be overheard. "Just between you and me, he'll receive a nice raise for being honest and reporting the problem instead of hiding it. Apparently, Dad had been looking to get rid of Josh for a while, so Henry blowing the whistle about the hours forgery gave him the reason he needed. Dad worried firing him for dating me would open him up to a lawsuit, which was news to me. But with the arrest and fraud, he was in the clear."

"He wanted to fire Josh for being your boyfriend?"

Elias's expression was a bit sheepish. "I assumed

he hated me being with Josh because he didn't like I was gay. It turns out the only thing that bothered him about our relationship was how miserable Josh made me. Since he was so hands-off while I was growing up, he didn't feel it was his place to interfere in my life and tell me who I shouldn't date, so he stayed silent. Dad's always been a workaholic who only cares about business, so I never thought that would matter to him. But I guess losing Mom forced him to reevaluate his relationship with me, he just hadn't figured out how to talk to me about it yet. We had a great conversation this afternoon after Josh was escorted off the premises."

I regretted not being there earlier, because I would have loved to have witnessed Josh getting thrown out once and for all. "It's great that you could reconcile with your dad. I'm relieved Josh won't be able to bother you anymore."

"None of this would have happened without the three of you helping me at the wedding." He smiled as he stood up to leave. "Anyway, I should let you get to your work."

If I was Jules, I would have hugged him, but I settled for telling him, "I'm glad we had the chance to talk. I'll be sure to give Jules his card when I see him again."

"I appreciate that. Have a great rest of the night, Xander."

"You, too." I waved as he left, my heart heavy

with sympathy over his loss and angry that Josh had used that to his advantage like the enormous asshole he was. I almost couldn't believe his actions were more despicable than I had originally thought, but he had proven himself to be the worst. Elias deserved genuine love, and not a bastard who was capitalizing on his grief just to use him. But at least now he would be free of Josh harassing him at the office.

I opened the envelope with my name on it and pulled out a card that had "Thank You" embossed on the front in silver-foil calligraphy. Inside was Elias's neatly written message.

> Xander,
>
> I don't know how I can ever thank you for what you've done for me. You had every reason to hate me because of Josh, but you helped save me from the worst mistake of my life. It sounds sad, but I hadn't realized how much I needed to hear that I deserved more than that until you told me.
>
> After seeing your wonderful relationship, I hope that I'm lucky enough to find my own Jules to love me the same way. Thank you for giving me the confidence that it might happen someday.

I can never repay you, Jules, or Callum for the kindness of offering me friendship and a place to belong despite everything. But please know that I am eternally grateful to all of you for helping me remember how to be happy again.

With sincerity and the deepest gratitude,
Elias Forthwright

My heart went out to him as I reread his note. I felt awful that in his time of need, he ended up with Josh, who probably made his grief even worse. All he wanted was for someone to love him, but he had ended up with an asshole who was incapable of it. It made me wish I knew someone who could be that perfect partner for Elias.

As I continued studying the note, I kept coming back to the line, "I hope that I'm lucky enough to find my own Jules to love me the same way."

We hadn't agreed to become a couple for real until after Elias left. But he had still seen the love between me and my best friend that had been apparent to everyone but us. Now that we had embraced it, it meant everything to me. I wanted that for Elias, especially after what he had been through.

A knock on my door drew my attention. I glanced up to find Jules standing there with a large paper bag and a smile, as if reading the card had summoned him. The cobalt-colored shirt and acid-washed blue jeans he wore brought out the color in his eyes. "Special delivery for my pookie." He shut the door behind him and locked it, making my heart skip a beat in a way it never had with Jules's previous work visits.

I could have kissed him for bringing something to eat after I had forgotten to. It was like he had a sixth sense about that kind of thing. "What's for dinner?"

"Chinese." He unloaded the bag onto my empty desk. "I ran into Elias in the elevator. It's amazing how different he is now from the guy I met Saturday."

I placed the thank-you card back in its envelope and set it aside with Jules's for later. "Did he tell you what happened to Josh today?"

Jules passed me chopsticks and cold sesame noodles, which were my favorite. He had his usual kung pao chicken. "No, but you know I love juicy office gossip. Spill it."

"He got fired this morning for forging his hours and getting arrested on Sunday."

My best friend stared at me with wide blue eyes. "You're joking, right? What did he get arrested for? Last time I checked, they couldn't arrest you just for being an asshole."

"It turns out he wasn't just two-timing me, he was three-timing me with the guy in charge of billable hours. They got into an ugly fight when Henry found out Josh was using him to inflate his hours, hoping to score that promotion. Cops showed up, and I can only imagine the attitude Josh took with them when he has enormous problems with authority. They hauled his ass to jail for disorderly conduct and assaulting an officer."

He moved the paper bag to the floor and sat down in the chair Elias had vacated. "Seriously?"

"Elias's dad fired Josh this morning. I'm annoyed I missed the showdown. It must have been spectacular."

"Well, good riddance to that asshole. I'm glad he won't be here to cause problems anymore." Jules took out a tea light candle and turned on the flickering LED flame before setting it between us on the desk.

I cocked an eyebrow at him. "A fake candle? Really?"

"It's fake because I wanted to add a little romance, not get lectured about fire safety."

I had to laugh at that, because I absolutely would have done that. "Fair enough. Thank you for the surprise romantic candlelit dinner." I opened the lid and began stirring the noodles in the sesame sauce. "How did you know I'd be here and hadn't eaten yet?"

He took his first bite of his meal. "Because you're you. You're incapable of taking a three-week vacation without stopping in to check on things. When you get fixated on your job, you forget to take care of yourself. You've been that way since forever. Well, it's either that, or I'm psychic. Take your pick."

"The irony is, I haven't done any work yet. Elias and I had a nice, long talk instead. He left this for you, by the way." I held up the envelope with his name on it before setting it aside for later. "It was a beautiful tradition with him and his mom. It's a shame he lost her so young, especially when they were so close. Meanwhile, my mother barely remembers I exist and will probably live to be one hundred and twenty-three by living off spite. It's not fair."

Both of my parents had neglected me in favor of the families they started with their second marriages. I hadn't heard from my dad because he'd cut all contact with me after the divorce when I was eight, and my mother had washed her hands of me the day I turned eighteen. If it weren't for Jules and his family, I would have had no one. I didn't care to think about it.

Jules pulled out two bottles of cold sparkling water from his messenger bag and passed one over to me. "Sorry, forgot about these. Anyway, let's not ruin dinner by talking about how much Eileen pisses me off. Tell me something good instead."

"Elias mentioned he hopes he can find his own Jules to love him the same way you love me. I thought it was sweet."

Jules grinned. "Too bad I don't have another brother. He deserves a boyfriend like that after what he's been through."

"It made me realize how lucky I am to be happy

with you now instead of wasting more years of my life being miserable with Josh."

"Aww, pookie." Jules blew me a kiss, making me laugh. "You say the sweetest things."

I took a sip of water, then savored another taste of my dinner. He had gotten it from our usual place, which had the best peanut-flavored sauce ever. "I've always been okay no matter what, because you were there for me. I never should have taken that for granted for so many years."

"The same is true in reverse."

"Yes, but you had your tight-knit family to support you," I pointed out.

He gave me the closest thing to a stern look he was capable of. "You've been the center of my universe since we were kids. Do you not understand I'd be lost without you?"

"That's not what I meant." I ate more of my noodles as I figured out what thought I wanted to express. "I guess what I'm trying to say is, I never want to take it for granted that you're my bunny who loves me."

His pleased smile was so beautiful, it made it worth it to admit such an embarrassing thing out loud. "You know the instant I finish this, I'm pouncing on you, right?"

"Mm-hmm. I'm looking forward to it."

True to his word, as soon as we finished dinner and put the containers back in the bag, he pinned me in my chair. "Do we finally get to do what everyone assumes we're doing behind your closed door?"

Given that it was almost nine o'clock at night, nobody would be on my floor at that hour. I never would have considered doing something so forbidden, but I had reevaluated my opinion after my experience with Jules in the supply closet at the reception. With my door locked, there was nothing stopping me from giving in to my naughty desires. "Today's your lucky day."

He leaned down to kiss me, allowing me to taste the lingering heat of his kung pao chicken. I didn't resist as he guided me out of my chair and repositioned us so I was resting my ass on the desk edge. "What do you want? Are you in the mood for me to bend you over and fuck you like I'll never see you again? Would you prefer to be flat on your back as I rail you? Or—"

I interrupted him with a hungry kiss. "Start with one, switch to two." I kicked off my shoes, building my excitement for what was about to happen.

"Got it." He roughly stripped me of my clothes. It aroused me, even as I had a moment of self-consciousness about being naked in my office for the first time in my life. He didn't give me long to think about it as he positioned me facedown on my desk. I heard him tear open a lube packet, before spreading my cheeks apart with his hands. I trembled with anticipation when a lubed finger slid into me, then two. He kept his pace slow and deliberate as he stretched me, building up my sexual frustration.

To distract me, he started asking questions. "Should I be your boss who's disciplining you for disappointing me? Maybe spank you as punishment for messing up something important?"

My professional pride made that an unworkable scenario. "We both know I'm too good of an employee for that, even in a fantasy."

"Do you want me to slap your ass, anyway?"

"Oh, fuck yes!" It was a pleasure I never imagined Jules would offer me. In the back of my mind, I had a slight concern that he would only want to make love to me now that we were together. That's why the thought of him hitting my ass made me almost impossibly hard. I wanted it so badly I couldn't stand the slow build up as a third finger breached me. "Fuck, I *need* it, Jules!"

"Patience." He took his time spreading me open, causing me to feel the total opposite instead. I pushed back against him, silently begging him for more. "Are you ready for me?"

"*Please!*" I whimpered when he withdrew his fingers in response. My muscles tensed in anticipation when I heard him strip off his shirt and pull down his zipper, then his pants and underwear. The slick sounds of him coating his cock with lube made me tremble. It took an effort to force my body to relax. "Don't hold back."

He slid his erection between my cheeks, then pressed closer to me to murmur in my ear, "How hard do you want it?"

"Make me scream."

"Are you sure?"

I rocked against him. "Yes!"

"As you wish."

He pushed into me, not stopping until he was balls-deep in me. It filled that ache inside me, but he was only getting started. There was nothing gentle about the way he used my body for his pleasure. Jules pounded into me rough and fast, which had me squirming under him from the intensity of it. He kept his left hand cupped against my neck, pinning me to the desk as he pounded into me. The aggressive fucking, devoid of any trace of tenderness, was even better after a weekend of him cherishing me with lovemaking.

"I want to hear you."

My soft groan didn't satisfy him.

"Not good enough." That was the only warning I got before he slapped my ass hard enough to make it sting. The burst of pleasure it sent exploding inside of me made me shout. "That's it. Let me hear that sexy voice of yours."

He repositioned my hips a little higher, allowing him to hit deeper. I gasped at the change, desperate for more.

"Come on, you can do better than that." When I

didn't comply, he spanked me again. I cried out as my body jerked under the harsh treatment, loving every second—until he slowed things down to an almost agonizing pace.

"No, please! I'm sorry, don't stop!" I was ready to say anything to make him go back to the earlier rhythm. "Julie!"

"Better." He started thrusting in deeper, but the unhurried pace was driving me nuts. "Keep going."

"Harder, damn it!"

"I'll give you what you need as soon as you give me what I want."

My lust made it easier to raise my voice to demand, "Fuck me, Julian!"

Without warning, he resumed his earlier roughness, slamming into me and making me shout again. He plowed me until I was weak in the knees, slapping my ass again. The satisfying tingle made my neglected cock desperate for attention. When I tried to fix that, Jules knocked my hand away.

I bristled over being denied. My growl of annoyance turned into a yelp when he bent my right arm behind my back and used it as leverage. It was the exact amount of hurt to feel good. My left hand gripped the desk edge as he fucked me so hard, I worried my computer monitor would fall over. It was the only thing keeping me upright when my knees buckled from the intense pleasure.

Without warning, he withdrew. The sudden loss

left me empty and in agony. Before I could complain, he forced me to turn over onto my back. The candle jabbed me in the shoulder with its pointed LED flame light bulb. "Ow! Damn it, Julian!"

When I knocked it onto the floor, he laughed. "Wow, now I'm *really* glad I brought a fake one."

"That would have earned you a second lecture on fire safety for sure." To refocus his attention, I wrapped my hand around my erection and stroked myself.

Hungry desire replaced his amusement as his gaze roamed over me. Satisfaction darkened his blue eyes, giving him an almost predatory expression. He pulled me closer to the edge of the desk, then spread my legs wider apart to expose all of me to him.

After pushing away my hand, he ghosted a single finger along the length of my erection. "Are you that ready for it to be over?"

"No, but I need more!"

He responded with a fierce kiss, devouring my mouth with shared passion. When he penetrated me once more, he spread my legs further apart to let him go deeper. I could only gasp and swear as I writhed on the desk from the ecstasy rocketing through my system. The tight way he gripped my thighs as he drove into me made it even better. I hoped it left bruises later. He dominated my desires until the only word I could remember was his name.

Jules guided my left leg over his shoulder, and my

right wound around his waist to keep in place as he hit the sweet spot inside me. It freed him up to take my hardness in hand and jerk me off as his hips continued pushing into me. "I want you to yell my name."

A few tugs were all I needed to oblige him as I arched off the desk, coming so hard that my seed splattered halfway up my chest. I moaned his name again when he climaxed inside me. Only then did we stop our frenetic fucking, both of us breathing heavily and sweating from the exertion. I pulled him down for a kiss, drowning in the taste of him. It was gentle compared to the harsher pleasure we had indulged in, but I enjoyed it all the same. Who knew office sex would be so enjoyable?

Adrift in the afterglow of such a satisfying release, I continued savoring the closeness between us. I was the luckiest man in the world to love my best friend, who would do anything to make me happy—including rough desk sex in my office. That level of ecstasy was worth putting up with embarrassing pet names.

After we cleaned up and put our clothes back on, Jules sat in my chair and pulled me to sit on his lap. He nuzzled against me with a kiss as he hugged me tight. It was a tender moment, which was why it startled me when he exclaimed, "Oh, the fortune cookies!"

Sometimes I suspected he enjoyed ordering

Chinese food so often because of them. He rolled us over so I could get them out of the bag. I handed him his, since he never picked his own. When we were younger, I'd test his patience by refusing to choose mine to see if he would take his first. He was too stubborn to crack under that pressure, so I caved every time. I had never understood why that was one of his quirks, but that was when the realization hit me. Turning to face him, I asked, "Do you never pick fortune cookies because of me?"

"What do you mean?"

The more I thought about what he said the day before, the more sense it made. "You've *always* insisted on me picking first. Do you do that because it gives me control over the decision, while also bossing you around into accepting the one I don't choose?"

His only response was a smile worthy of the Cheshire cat.

"I get to be selfish and capriciously decide which is mine, which dictates what you end up with and forces you to humor my whims. It ticks all your boxes." The revelation stunned me. "Wow, you *really* weren't kidding when you said you liked my authoritative streak, were you?"

"Nope." Rather than being embarrassed, he radiated amusement over me figuring out the secret of his fortune cookie quirk. "It goes far beyond liking it."

"But that doesn't make sense!" I kept trying to piece it together and failing. "You were chaos personified as a kid. If you didn't want to do something, nothing in the world could make you do it. It drove your parents nuts that you only did what you were told if it was something you felt like doing. You never gave a shit about anyone's authority, because you live by your own rules. You've broken up with boyfriends because they became too controlling. My domineering personality is the antithesis of all that, so why do you like it?"

"Because out of everything you've ever asked for, you've never demanded I be perfect or be anyone other than who I am. Not once." He caressed my cheek with such a loving expression it made me feel choked up. "When we were kids, I was the total opposite of you. You needed perfect grades; I didn't care. Your room was so clean, it could have been in an interior design magazine; mine looked like a bomb exploded. Your perfectionism required everything to be ordered and precise; I was so wild that I was incapable of that. But you were still my friend despite all of that. If anything, you should have hated me."

It was all true. "You definitely overwhelmed me at first."

"And you baffled the shit out of me." We laughed before he continued. "But I was drawn to your calmness, your rational mind, your organized method of handling things, because I needed that to stop me from spinning out into a disaster. I trusted you and your perfectionism to keep me in line. That's why you were the only person I listened to back then and now."

"I would have been unbearable without you. You're the one who taught me to loosen up and have fun. You're also the only person who told me it was okay to be sad." He hugged me tighter, which made me feel better. "It works because we balance each other out."

Jules nodded in agreement. "Exactly."

"So, should we see what our fortune cookies say about it?" I opened mine, then pulled out the paper to read it out loud. "Mine says, 'You will learn an important secret about a loved one today.' Wow."

He laughed in disbelief. "Seriously?"

To prove it, I held it up to show him. "One hundred percent true."

"Are you positive you want to eat that fortune cookie? It's damn near sentient."

"I'll take my chances." I ate it without remorse. "Mmm, who knew sentient tasted so delicious? What's yours say?"

Jules opened his and removed his fortune. "Ooh, mine's excellent. It says, 'You will soon discover new pleasures in bed.'"

He had always had a thing about adding "in bed" to the end of fortunes. His theory was it improved every fortune and worked with most of them. It was stupid, but it made me laugh. "No, it doesn't. Let me see." To my surprise, it actually said that, minus the "in bed" part.

"You know what this means, don't you?" His smirk was wicked and beautiful.

I feigned innocence. "It's time for you to leave, so I can get to work?"

"Nope, you're coming home with me and we're taking a second shot at finding out how much I enjoy being bossed around by you in bed."

"What if I say no?"

"Sorry, but fortune cookie law mandates we must obey it. It's the only other thing I listen to besides you."

It was fun playing along with his game. "I hate to break it to you, but you're violating the primary statute."

"Which is?"

"If you don't eat the fortune cookie, your fortune doesn't come true."

He popped half of his fortune cookie into his mouth with a grin. "Already on it, boss."

I might have liked him calling me "boss" more than I enjoyed being "sir" last time. That was something we would have to try out once we got back to his apartment. "Eager?"

Jules finished the other half. "Hell yeah."

"Then let's go."

Chapter Fourteen
JULES

TO CELEBRATE Xander staying out of his office for the entire week, I took him to Ambrosia. It was a two-star Michelin restaurant run by our friend, Maria, and her wife, Renée, who was the head chef. There was a private area in the back where they entertained special guests, which was where we always preferred to eat. It was like a beautiful Garden of Eden just for us.

At night, it was even more magical because of the fairy lights that wrapped around the wooden pergola and flower-covered trellis. We could faintly hear the din of the restaurant and the quiet burbling of a marble fountain. It made Sunnyside feel a million miles away instead of outside the stone walls and locked gate.

After knowing Maria and Renée for years, they had very strong opinions about me and Xander being together. They thought I was a lovable idiot for not being honest with myself or him. I had endured a fair amount of ball-busting over it, especially from Renée. I was curious to see how they would react now that we were dating for real.

However, after enjoying five dishes of our six-course dinner, Maria hadn't made a single comment about our relationship. I asked Xander, "Is it weirding you out that we've almost finished and Maria hasn't commented about us? Because it's kind of bothering me."

He rolled his eyes. "You finally have a meal where you're spared some ribbing at your expense, and now you're complaining about it?"

It sounded stupid when he put it that way. "I'm just saying it feels strange that she's not teasing me about you. It's almost making me feel like I miss it, which is nuts."

"Incredibly." Xander hid his smile by taking a sip of his wine.

Maria returned with a server to clear our plates and deliver our last dessert course. She was a former model who was tall, elegant, and full of grace. She styled her brunette hair in its usual updo, with a glittering pin holding it in place. Her purple-and-red dress emphasized her curves, and her ever-present smile was bright and cheery. It was highly suspicious.

After the server cleared out empty plates from the prior course, Maria placed our desserts on the table. It looked like a crystal snow globe on top of cake, with something white, a leafy green, and a purple flower inside. It was almost too beautiful to eat. Renée had outdone herself yet again.

"For dessert, this is an apple pie and cinnamon parfait."

Her simple description and the stunning work of art on the table didn't match. "How is *this* an apple pie? It has a crystal ball on it!"

"It's actually an isomalt ball," Maria said, as if I had any clue what that was. "Aka a sugar globe. It's fun to shatter with your spoon so you can eat it. There's a gingersnap crumble on the bottom and apple pie filling, with mint and violas to top off the cinnamon parfait."

I turned my plate to appreciate the dessert from different angles. It was remarkable that something so beautiful could also be edible. "Where does Renée come up with this kind of stuff?"

Maria shrugged. "No clue."

Xander continued studying his. "How did she create the dome?"

"She has a hand pump to blow air into it with the same technique glassblowers use. I've watched her do it countless times, and I never stop being amazed by it. Plus, anytime she breaks out the blowtorch, it's guaranteed to be awesome."

"What part of this required a blowtorch?"

"She uses it to heat up the ring to cut a hole in the bottom of the ball."

That sounded like my kind of mayhem, which was why Xander frowned with disapproval. "The absolute last thing you need in the kitchen is a blowtorch. You'd burn the entire apartment building down trying to make crème brûlée."

He wasn't wrong. "You honestly believe I'm ambitious enough to try that? At best, I'd start with roasting marshmallows."

"Either way, it ends with the fire department being called."

There was no defense to that, given my culinary propensity for catching shit on fire. Our exchange would ordinarily earn us some choice comments, but Maria remained silent as she observed with a serene smile. I couldn't take it anymore, so I called her out on it. "Okay, you're officially weirding me out. Why aren't you saying anything about us?"

"Like what?" she innocently asked. I knew her better than that.

"At the very least, you'd normally comment, 'If you admitted how you felt about Xander, I'm sure he'd be happy to make you dessert without setting off the fire alarm.' But you haven't said a word."

"Aww, that's so cute. I didn't realize you missed my teasing."

Her reaction confirmed something was up. "I'm more confused than anything."

"Now, what reason would I possibly have to quit bothering you about being with Xander?" She tapped her chin as she pretended to think. "I'll let you boys ponder over that while you enjoy dessert."

With that, she walked away with an enigmatic smile that made me want to groan. Maria and Renée could be so damn cryptic sometimes.

I picked up my spoon, only to receive a warning. "If you want Rune to cook anything for you again, you'll take a picture first and then a video of you breaking the sugar globe for him and Callum."

My brother and his boyfriend were also close friends with Renée and Maria. Rune loved cooking and Callum adored desserts, so they both would love to see this masterpiece. I pulled out my phone to snap a few pictures to send to them later. "Thank you for the reminder, pookie. Even though we both know you would have taken photos and a video of yours as a backup if I forgot."

I switched over to record a video. Unsure of how hard I should hit it, I decided a good whack would ensure the best results. When I cracked it with my spoon, the ball splintered and shattered into crystalline shards that made the dessert beautiful in a new way. It was spectacularly dramatic. Stopping my video, I snapped one last photo of the aftermath before putting my phone away. "More desserts should include wanton destruction. That's incredibly satisfying."

"Check your photos and video to make sure they're good before I do mine."

Thank god one of us was an adult. I did as he suggested, pleased to discover I had done an outstanding job. When I showed him the results, he nodded in satisfaction. He then cracked his sugar dome, which broke apart and scattered over his dish. "Damn, that *is* fun."

"I'll send the pictures after I tell them how amazing it tastes." With my phone put away again, I sampled the dessert. Even though it looked nothing like the apple pie it claimed to be, the flavors of the crumble and filling were spot-on in resemblance. It was perfection when mixed with the cinnamon parfait and crunchy sugar, which balanced everything. "Wow, this is unreal." I ate another bite, savoring the spices that added a little kick to it.

Xander moaned in appreciation, the sound going straight to my dick. The euphoric expression on his face as he swallowed only made it worse.

I shifted in my seat. "Is there some reason you're trying to give me a hard-on?"

His knowing grin told me he was very aware of what he was doing. "You mean I haven't succeeded yet?"

"Do you want me to pull you across this table and graphically demonstrate the nature of our relationship for them?"

"Can you at least wait until I've finished this dessert?"

It seemed another round of Questions was in order. "Can you eat faster?"

"Are you that eager?"

I couldn't help egging him on. "To make love to you on this cast-iron table outside in a garden?"

"Think we could finish before they came to check on us?"

"Do you want to find out?" I sure as hell did.

"What do you think?"

When Xander sucked on his spoon suggestively, it completely derailed my train of thought. "You know that's cheating, right?"

I wanted to kiss the cocky grin off his gorgeous face. "Does that mean it's working?" He deliberately did it again, which put me in genuine danger of getting aroused before Renée came out to say hello. There was no need to give her quite that much ammo to tease me with.

"Just wait until later."

He became triumphant. "Ha, I win! That's not a question."

I looked at him with all the desire I was trying to hold back for him. "Yeah, you're right. It's a fucking promise."

The visible shiver my words sent through him only made me want more. I had to check myself and remember to eat my dessert. It was by far the best tasting and most artistic apple pie I had ever enjoyed in my life, and I didn't want to waste it.

Realizing we both needed to cool off, Xander switched topics. "You know, it really says a lot that I've stayed out of the office this entire week because of you."

"I'm so glad sex with me is better than doing paperwork."

We shared a laugh. "That, and it's been fun being this relaxed all the time. I'm used to always being tightly wound, but being here with you tonight, I'm not stressed at all right now. Minus the part where I thought about you using a blowtorch in my kitchen, of course."

"Of course." I grinned. "Are you about to turn into a schmoopy mookie-pookie bear on me?"

He attempted to scowl in annoyance, but it was difficult when he was fighting back laughter. "Why don't you be a good bunny and eat your flower instead of being such a smart-ass?"

I picked up the viola and pretended to nibble on it like a rabbit, causing him to laugh. To my surprise, it tasted great because of the sugar dusting on its delicate petals. I ate it for real, earning me an arched eyebrow. "What? It's delicious."

"Is that your inner bunny talking?" He nudged his with his spoon. It and the mint leaves were the last things left on his plate.

"Seriously, try it."

I couldn't blame him for looking at it with suspicion, but he ate it with a surprised noise. "Wow, is there anything she can't make taste incredible?"

It startled us when Renée answered, "Durian fruit." She had come out with Maria, who was masking her amused expression behind her hand. I had no idea when they had arrived, but I was sure they had seen more than I wanted them to.

While Maria was elegant, Renée was rougher around the edges. It was the classic opposites attract, but they balanced each other out in perfect harmony. Renée's blond hair was shaved on the sides and left long on top in rainbow stripes. Her arms, hands, and neck were covered in tattoos, most of which were culinary in theme. She was in her chef whites, emblazoned with the restaurant logo and two stars to represent the honor of earning her Michelin rating.

Ignoring that they had caught us in the middle of some bizarre flirting, I asked, "What's that?"

"It's an Asian fruit that looks like a giant, spiky testicle and smells like a combination of turpentine, onions, raw sewage, and gym socks." Renée hugged Xander hello before giving me one next. As a fellow hugger, she always gave great, hearty ones that told you how glad she was to see you. "Or, as Anthony Bourdain described it, 'your breath will smell as if you'd been french-kissing your dead grandmother' after you eat it."

I struggled not to gag at the very vivid description. "And people eat that?"

"Yeah, especially in desserts, which is mind-blowing. Although, you get fined for eating it on mass transport in Singapore because the rotting meat stench is too potent for such an enclosed space. It's so bad, they've had to evacuate buildings because someone ate one." Renée wrinkled her nose. "There're ways of cooking it to make it sweet, but the scent is too off-putting in the process, not to mention the awful aftertaste that hits afterward. It's one of the few things I won't touch. I don't care how delicious the dessert is; I don't want my mouth to taste or smell like a reanimated corpse."

Out of all the conversations I thought I'd have with Renée, talking about tasting dead bodies on your breath was not one of them. "On behalf of my stomach and nose, thank you. More importantly, thanks for the incredible apple pie. If you don't make that for Rune and Callum sometime, they'll be devastated."

"Do you really think I'd miss out on Callum losing his shit over it?" He had quickly become one of Renée's favorite people because of his genuine and enthusiastic appreciation for everything she cooked. The nicest compliment I had ever heard her give was saying his reactions reminded her of why being a chef was her dream job. He was the sole exception she made with going out to the garden to personally deliver dessert instead of waiting to visit after the meal finished. She loved watching him take his first bite and seeing his unfiltered joy. "I suspect as soon as the term is over, they'll be here to celebrate."

Not wanting to ruin Renée's fun, I asked, "So I shouldn't send the pictures and video I took of tonight's dessert to them?"

"Wouldn't you rather torture them with tales about my magical dessert that you're dying to tell them about, but they have to see it for themselves to believe?" Her grin was wicked. It was one of the countless reasons I enjoyed being around her. "You know how much Rune *loves* cryptic comments."

"You're right, as always." The woman had an uncanny ability to cut through layers of bullshit to the truth.

"And yet it took you two this many years to start fucking," Renée said with a tut as she gestured between me and Xander.

Maria facepalmed beside her with a groan. "Sometimes a *little* subtlety wouldn't hurt, honey."

"Pfft, what's the fun in that? After I've spent so long busting their balls about their feelings, I'm allowed to gloat." She beamed with pride. "Good for you. It's about damn time."

"All jokes aside, we really are happy for you both," Maria added.

"Especially now that I know you're Xander's cute little bunbun. Thanks for an entertaining new thing to poke fun at you about." Renée cooed as she stroked under my chin like I was a bunny.

His eyes lit up with delight that promised I was in for some trouble later. "*Bunbun?*"

I glanced up at her with mild exasperation. "Thanks for that."

"You're welcome. Personally, I think it suits you quite nicely." She looked at me with warm fondness, which took the sting out of my minor annoyance.

"What gave us away?"

Maria answered first. "You're finally at peace."

"Which is her polite way of saying it's obvious the two of you have——"

"*Renée.*"

She held up her hands in surrender. "Fine. We all get the picture without me spelling it out. What I want to know is how did it happen? Was it a dramatic you couldn't take it anymore and just had at it situation? Was it celebratory breakup sex over Xander finally dumping Josh? Or were you bored and fooled around for fun, then your feelings came out?"

"I believe it all started with 'Shut up and hug me.' Isn't that right, pookie?" I made a kissy face at him, causing Renée to giggle. Two could play at that game.

"*Pookie?*" She was downright gleeful over the moniker. "Oh, it's so nauseatingly saccharine! I love it!"

Xander gave me a look that promised I'd be paying for that later, but it was worth it.

Renée wrapped an arm around her wife's waist and pulled her closer. "I need to step up my pet name game."

Maria looked up at the sky with a long-suffering sigh. "God help me." Her mock despair was quickly replaced with a playful challenge. "Keep in mind that turnabout is fair play. If you come up with a terrible nickname for me, I'll get revenge. Choose wisely."

"Oh, this will be *so* much fun."

"You're going to torment me with this, aren't you?"

Renée grinned. "Absolutely."

"Remember, payback's a bitch, sweetie."

"Totally worth it." The expression of love between them said a lot. "Well, I should stop playing and get back in the kitchen. Thank you for *finally* coming to your senses, you two. It sure took you long enough."

I couldn't be mad at her when her heart was in the right place. It made me realize something important. "Now that we're together, you're going to switch to teasing us about when we're getting married, aren't you?"

Renée did her best impression of an innocent look. "Me? Tease you? Why, I've never heard of such an outlandish thing in all my life."

"Uh-huh. Sure. That's totally believable. Yep."

I stood up to give Maria a proper hug goodbye. She teased, "Hey, you're the one who missed me joking with you about it. I have to make up for lost time with at least a few engagement jokes to maintain my reputation."

Renée came over and hugged me next. She said for my ears only, "I'm proud of you for deciding to be with him."

"What makes you assume it didn't happen the other way around?"

"Because it's obvious who calls the shots between you two." She gave me a flirty wink when she pulled back. "Enjoy being happy. You both deserve that."

I held her gaze as I replied, "Thank you, Renée."

She patted my cheek fondly, understanding that I meant so much more than just gratitude over our superb dinner. "You're welcome, Jules."

After a few more parting words, they returned inside, leaving me and Xander alone once more. He came over to stand in front of me, looking up as he tried to smother a grin. "You know what you're stuck with for life, don't you?"

I reached out and pulled him closer into my embrace. "You?"

"Me," he said, giving me a teasing kiss before adding, "and bunbun."

"I can live with that." Our next kiss was more heated as we held each other. I tried not to think about Marie and Renée watching us from inside the restaurant. "Why don't we go home, and I'll show you what an insatiable bunny I can be?"

"*Bunbun!*" The delight Xander took in the silly name was charming.

"Hey, that's Mr. Bunbun Foo Foo to you."

His peals of laughter made my soul happy. "Well, come along, Mr. Bunbun Foo Foo. I believe you have some bopping on the head to do when we get home."

"I'm looking forward to it." Not only to that but spending the rest of my life in love with my best friend.

Epilogue
XANDER

ONE MONTH LATER

THERE WERE a lot of wonderful aspects about dating your best friend. Besides the fact Jules knew me inside and out, we could sit in comfortable silence without it being awkward. I had been taking care of emails for work on my computer from the oversized chair in Jules's apartment, while he sketched on his tablet. He was a talented artist, and I loved seeing his art. While he worked as a graphic designer, he also was a very skilled illustrator.

After wrapping up a few more things online, I closed my laptop and set it on the side table. Since I had nothing else better to do, I enjoyed watching Jules work. His white pajama pants covered in a pattern saying "I'm bananas for you" with two bananas hugging was so perfectly him. Absorbed in what he was doing, he didn't look up at all as he continued drawing. I was curious what he was working on so intently, but I refused to disturb him.

Even though he never lifted his gaze from his screen, Jules said, "I can feel you watching me."

"Should I stop?"

The corners of his mouth turned up in a smile, but he still didn't glance my way. "It makes me want to put on a show for you."

"I'm not an artist, but I'm pretty sure it's impossible to strip and draw at the same time."

He chuckled as his hand continued moving. "That almost sounds like a challenge."

"I can go take a shower if you prefer to focus on finishing."

"Yeah, like I'd really be able to concentrate when you're naked in my shower." He finally looked up at me. "Do you want to come over here and give me your opinion?"

Pleased by the invite, I moved to curl up next to him on the couch. On his screen was a cartoon drawing of a pastel blue bunny and a lavender "caticorn," which was a cat with a rainbow gradient unicorn horn and tail. They both had pink hearts on their cheeks instead of whiskers, with smiles on their faces. It was a precious image, and if I was anyone else, I would have cooed out loud at the cuteness. "Wow, that's adorable." I kissed his cheek. "I never cease to be amazed at how talented you are."

"It's nice to be reminded sometimes." He changed the perspective to let me see the details of the two figures, which somehow was more precious up close. "I mentioned it as a joke before, but I might be onto something with this idea."

He zoomed all the way out, revealing the title, *Pookie & Bunbun in Love*. "I want to turn it into a webcomic series. What do you think?"

"As cute as it is, you'll have a million followers by Friday."

My comment made him chuckle as he tweaked Bunbun's paw with the stylus to round it out more before saving the file. "I appreciate the vote of confidence, but that seems ambitious, even for me. If the names bother you, I can change them."

"It's perfect." Turning his head, I guided him closer for a gentle kiss. "Am I a unicorn kitten because I only want attention when it suits me?"

"No, it's because you're super cute, a little magical, and I love cuddling you." He wrapped an arm around me to hold me close. "And maybe it's a subconscious passive-aggressive suggestion that we should adopt one together when you move in after your lease is up in three months."

The idea filled me with joy. "You mean adopt two. Life is better when you have your best friend with you, even when you're cats."

"You're right." Jules pressed a kiss against my forehead. "I couldn't have said it better myself."

Because I was well-acquainted with how Jules's mind worked, I preemptively shut down a suggestion I knew was coming. "And no, we're not naming one of them Meatball."

He pretended to act disappointed. "But what if he's a tubby little chonk?"

"Doesn't matter."

Julian took great pleasure in reminding me, "For the record, you brought up 'meatball' as a nickname first. You have nobody to blame for that but yourself."

He was right, but I didn't have to admit it. "How about that shower?" I also wasn't above petty tactics like that to save myself from losing.

Jules flipped the case cover closed. When he put it and the digital pencil on the coffee table, my excitement spiked. "That's a great idea."

I got off the couch and held out my hand to help him stand up. "Hop along, bunbun. It's time to get naked."

The desire in his blue eyes sent fire racing through my veins. "Lead the way, pookie."

I laughed as we headed to his shower, where Jules proved to me all over again why choosing to be happy with him was my greatest decision. Jules wasn't just my best friend. He was my family, my home, and the greatest love of my life. Because he was my entire world and happy ever after, I could excuse myself for becoming schmaltzy enough to unironically call him my bunbun without embarrassment. There was no greater testament to how much I loved him than that.

What important question does Jules have to ask Xander before their first anniversary romantic getaway? **Claim your copy of Bestest Friend to find out today**.

Want to see Elias get the happily ever after he deserves now that he's free from his awful ex-boyfriend? **Read Love Directions next to enjoy his heartwarming HEA**.

Want to see where the Sunnyside universe begins? **Check out Bet on Love to start the adventure**.

Thank You

Thank you for reading **Love Fool**. Reviews are crucial for helping other readers discover new books to enjoy. If you want to share your love for Jules and Xander, please leave a review. I'd really appreciate it!

Recommending my work to others is also a huge help. Don't hesitate to give this book a shout-out in your favorite book rec group to spread the word.

About the Series

If you want to see more of Jules and Xander's story, you can read an exclusive bonus chapter if you join my newsletter.

The fifth book of this series is **Love Directions**. It focuses on Elias's romance with North Easton, who is Callum's friend and Felix's roommate from Chapter 8 of **Fancy Love**. Several other characters from previous books appear in it as well. If this is your first book in the **Good Bad Idea** series, I'd definitely recommend checking out **Bet on Love** to see where all the fun begins.

Love Directions is a very touching love story, so if you enjoyed Callum's sweetness, you're going to adore watching Elias on his journey. It's a cute insta love, shy/flirt, opposites attract, gay romance that will get you right in the feels with its heartfelt story.

To stay up to date on the latest series news, please be sure to subscribe to my newsletter, follow me on Twitter and Instagram, or join my Facebook group, Ariella Zoelle's Sunnyside. I do exclusive previews every Teaser Tuesday and WIP Wednesday, so please come join us if you want a glimpse at what I'm working on for the future.

Next in Series

AVAILABLE NOW

A playful flirt like North never expects to fall in love with a shy sweetheart like Elias. But what's more fun than an unexpected romance between two total opposites who fall in love at first sight?

Elias Forthwright

As someone who is painfully shy, I never expected to be attracted to a man like North. Not only is he younger than me, but he's the "flirty life of the party" type who tells the best stories. Someone as vivacious and bombastic as him would normally never notice a quiet attorney like me, right? But when it feels fate brought him into my life for a reason exactly when I needed him the most, I want to believe his declaration that he really desires me.

I've always lived my life taking the safe bet, but just this once, I want to be bold and do something wild. Isn't taking a leap of faith to fall in love with North worth the risk if it leads me into his arms and a lifetime of happiness?

North Easton

I'm an unapologetic hedonist, so I normally hook up with hot frat guys who are only interested in having a good time. Relationships are the last thing on my mind because I'm too busy having fun. I never in a million years expected to fall in love at first sight with a shy sweetheart who makes me want to believe in the happily-ever-afters I write about in my gay romance novels. But Elias is everything I never knew I wanted. And maybe this is a bad idea, but I don't just want him. I *need* him.

After everything Elias has been through lately, I'm determined to give him all the love he deserves while making him laugh. Even though we're polar opposites and literally just met, all the signs point to him being the one. Who am I to turn down an awesome gift like him from the cosmic universe?

Love Directions is the fifth book in the ***Good Bad Idea*** series and part of the Sunnyside universe. This novel features an insta love, shy/flirt, opposites attract, gay romance. If you love cute sweetness, sexy fun, and low angst stories that will make you laugh and swoon, you'll adore this satisfying HEA without cliffhangers. Each book can be read as a standalone or as part of the series in order.

Also by Ariella Zoelle

For a complete and up-to-date list of Ariella Zoelle's low angst releases, please visit her website at

www.ariellazoelle.com/ariella-zoelle-all

Also by A.F. Zoelle

In the mood for something with more angst and drama? Check out A.F. Zoelle's dark romances at

www.ariellazoelle.com/af-zoelle-all

Acknowledgments

First and foremost, thank you to all of you who have taken the time to share your excitement and passion for my **Good Bad Idea** series. While this has been one of the most trying and difficult years for me in some respects, it has also been the best because I've been lucky enough to connect with my readers. It means everything to me that people are enjoying these books as much as I'm having fun writing them.

Writing this book gave me extra warm fuzzies for my friends, who have been so wonderfully supportive during this time of transition for me. I'm so lucky to have their love and support. I never would have managed to get this book out in time without Nena and Chris's help with my recent move.

I'm so appreciative that Pam and Sandra have made it possible to get these books out every two months. It's a big ask, and they step up every time.

I also want to thank Katie from Gay Romance Reviews and all of the ARC readers who have touched me with their kind encouragement! Many of the reviews have been wonderfully encouraging, so I save them to enjoy on rough days.

I can't wait to meet again in **Love Directions**!

About the Author

ariella zoelle
WWW.ARIELLAZOELLE.COM

Ariella Zoelle adores steamy, funny, swoony romances where couples are allowed to just be happy. She writes low angst stories full of heat, humor, and heart. But sometimes she's in the mood for something with a bit more angst and drama. If you are too, check out her A.F. Zoelle books.

Get a bonus chapter by using the QR code below!

Printed in Great Britain
by Amazon